THE UNFOLDING

JEEHAN QUIJANO

THE UNFOLDING

LIBRARY OF CONGRESS CATALOGING-IN-PUBLICATION DATA

The Unfolding
Authored by Jeehan Quijano

ISBN: 9780999461723
LCCN: 2018939236

For my Dad

PROLOGUE

"IN THE BEGINNING, *there was only the sky and the sea, and between them was a hawk. One day the hawk roused the sea until it burst its waters against the sky. The sky reacted by creating many islands so the sea could no longer rise. Then the sky told the hawk to build her nest on the islands and leave the sky and the sea alone. The hawk was now glad that there was land.*

At this time the marriage of the land-breeze and the sea-breeze took place. They had a child—a bamboo. One day, the bamboo struck the feet of the hawk. This made the hawk mad and she pecked the bamboo until it slit open in two. From one section there emerged a man, and from the other, a woman.

Then the earthquake asked what should be done with the man and the woman. The birds and the fishes said that they should marry, and so it was done. The couple bore many children.

After some time, the parents grew tired of their idle and restless children and thought of a place where they could send them. More time passed, and the children grew in number and the parents became very weary at the lack of peace. Desperate and anxious, the father got hold of a stick and began beating the children.

The children got scared and dashed off in different directions. Some hid behind the walls, and some sought shelter inside the rooms. *Some ran to the fireplace, others ran outside. And there are those who fled to the sea.*

Now it turned out that those who went into the hidden rooms became the chiefs of the islands, and those who hid behind the walls became slaves. Those who ran outside became free men, and those who hid in the fireplace became dark skinned people. Those who went to the sea were absent for a very long time. And when they came back, they became the white people."

"Bamboo? Why a bamboo? Why not something else?"

"I don't know. It's a Filipino myth that began a long, long time ago, and since then has been passed on from one generation to another. Don't ask so many questions. When my father told me that story I was a boy your age, and he told me to remember it so that I can pass it on to my future children so now I am sharing it with you. One day when you become a father then you can tell the same story to your children. There's another thing about bamboos that I can tell you."

"Tell me, papa."

"The bamboo that your mother planted a long time ago flowered yesterday. Now that is a rare occurrence. They say that it happens very few times every one hundred years or so. And when it happens, bamboo plants of the same species blossom at the same time all over the world."

"The world? Like America?"

"Sure. But you know what the best part is?"

"I don't know."

"They say that the flowering is a sign of good news or good luck. I hope it's true, son. We need luck, just one bit of good luck in this lifetime. But where did you hear about America, son?"

"*Manong* Sergio's daughter, Carmela, married her pen pal from America. And she lives there now. She sends a *balikbayan* box full of goodies twice a year. And money for her brothers to go to school. I want to go to America someday, papa, and send you a lot of money and build you a big house with plenty of big rooms and a huge backyard for the chickens. And the backyard will be so big that you can plant whatever you like in there."

"I don't know anything about America, but what I do know is that you can never tell what a person's destiny will be, Benjamin."

PART ONE

1

NO BODY HAS ARRIVED YET. NO FUCKING BODY.

There was no telling that they were walking all over their
graves. One morning, rains equal to a month's fall poured
angrily for five hours and swept the city; the water swelled
and soared and towered beyond the concrete. The river gushed
through the streets and alleys until everything dry became
wet. Roofs were made into makeshift boats and anywhere you
turned, there was only water. Mud and debris joined the swirl
and human sounds became faint against the wind's battering
and the water's billow. After the weather mellowed, mud-cov-
ered bodies turned up on the streets. Everyone suffered an
equal fate from the reckless typhoon. It is rumored that Don
Rafael is among the thousands stranded along Avenue 9 in
Calamba city, a three-hour flight from San Jacinto. I was told
that he may be one of the casualties, and if this is indeed true,
then one could say that he died a lonely death, just another
statistic in the body count.

This was not how I conceived that Don Rafael would meet
his death. I imagined a gun pointed at his temple where upon
he would beg for mercy, or through food poisoning, as is often
the case in the barrios. Men like him do not pass away from
old age, as there will always be people plotting his death, even

if only in their minds. I want to take the life of my benefactor and I know I can do it triumphantly. Most would find it strange that I occupy my thoughts with retribution. That I, the once lowly lad he mentored, has turned into a brute. Such a loathsome ingrate, people will accuse me. But I do not care. I am a battered man living on the edge. I am beyond myself, beyond canons and moral convictions.

SAN JACINTO, A FLAT TERRAIN of vast sugar cane plantations, is the place of beginnings, of my first acquaintance with the Don. The scanty nipa hut where my family used to live is still in place. Stories were born there, and when you linger for a while by the propped-up swinging shades of the window, you'd know that dreams were bred there too. It was home to my parents before I was born. Constantly repaired over time, it was passed on to my father by his father, a dwelling unfit for a family of more than two, inadequate not only because of its puny size but also due to the inferior quality of its materials and foundations. Such is the fate of my kind—born indigent and destined to die as one. But in the hour when I was born, unexpected rain fell, and if I were to believe my mother's alleged foreboding, that strange rainfall on that summer morning of my birth was a portent of what she called my unusual lot. What she spoke of then, I suppose, is where I am now, a man who has moved up in the world, far better than I ever was, beyond a leaking roof and torn slippers, past poverty and hopelessness.

You would think that the town is laidback, even lifeless. Nothing stirs but the day's passing. Slack mornings, silvery evenings. But somewhere along the prolific farmland that lies in between the far mountains on one end, and the Pacific

Ocean on the other, the embers tarry, ready to ignite fire if provoked. No one questions how the embers came about, as it is part of history, like God and the gods. But once a week, on Sundays, the town turns into a circus. When the church bells chime, it is the time for commonplace gatherings. The townsfolk step out from their dwellings to assemble at the age-old church that the Spaniards built. The parish priest gives his sermon; people are relieved to hear words that have to do with salvation and the rewards awaiting them in heaven. Hallelujahs are proclaimed. Then the Catholic populace wanders about the town square with delighted faces. The men drink palm wine with their *compadres*, the women gossip and head to the flea market. When the multitude assembles on this day, the town turns into a place of rhetoric. A few gab and gab, while the majority nod and nod. The church bells chime again for the *Angelus*, pensive; it is sundown. On this day of the week, children are children until dusk. People go home and carry with them all sorts of torches. It is a day like any other, like the previous days of previous years. But you will be deceived. For the generation before this one unwittingly passed on a millstone. Unlike other histories, the history of the soul is private; no one knows the precise account of its journeys until you hear—He lost it? *Ay Diyos Santo!* Lord have mercy!—the nervous exclamations that incite prying. Disbelief, numbness, aggravation—who knew such a flurry of sentiments could be stimulated from within a drowsy town?

What Don Rafael was doing in Calamba city on the day of the wild storm is anyone's guess. Some say he was there to meet someone. They do not know who, but someone important, someone who could help him get out of a delicate situation. Some believe he skipped town because he had a premonition that he was going to get into an accident in San Jacinto. Others claim that he deliberately fled and any news of his death is merely a ploy. They say that he is in hiding; that he is, in fact, alive and well.

Is he? There is nothing more I desire right now than to see his body, to spit on it if dead, and if alive, to extinguish its last breath with my own hands.

2

I MAY HAVE ROMANTICIZED Don Rafael Garcia Madrigal. I was credulous. When I was a child I imagined a world to my liking, one that was good and benevolent. Perhaps that was my folly.

I bowed, naturally, to the man whom everyone addressed as Don, a title bestowed only to the privileged, a Spanish *mestizo* with light brown hair, thin nose and lips. Born to entitlement. As a dark brown, flat-nosed inferior boy with nothing to my name, I did not dare inquire about the sudden turn of events that led me to that big house, and to him, the man, the catalyst of it all.

Come along, Benjamin, walk with me, a nudge for a stroll on his estate, an old drab mansion that sat on a sprawling landscape of manicured land, the place where our arrangement came to fruition. My residence there was not very unusual as it was common for servants, young and old, to live on the estate, in a separate wing behind the main house. I anticipated at the beginning that I was to be an errand boy paid at month's end, just like the rest of the servants.

"How old are you, Benjamin? Ten? Nine?

"Nine, sir."

"Ah, had my son lived, he would have been your age. Come have *merienda* with me."

I obliged, of course, to the man who invited me to his home, who was mindful not to chide, who spoke to me like a son. I praised his kindness and did not find him patronizing. I was incapable of suspicion. I was a child of commoners and considered myself lucky to be standing there, being spoken to, listened to, by the god of our town.

"Do you want to go to school? You must. It is important to have education in this world. It will ensure you a better quality of life. Besides, it's the one thing that no one can take away from you. Do you have any aspirations? Do you want to be a doctor? Engineer? Policeman? Teacher? Surely there must be something. Or perhaps you want to experience what it's like to be away from the farm. Maybe go to the city. There is much more to life than what is in San Jacinto. The farm will always be there, you see. But opportunities in life don't come often, if at all. You do want to go to school, don't you?"

"Yes, sir, I do. Oh, I want that very much."

"Then it shall be arranged! I will waste no time making sure that you get all the chances and help you need and that this takes place immediately. Prepare yourself. It is going to be an adventure for you. In the meantime, I want you to feel comfortable here, get acquainted with everyone. Do not be shy around me, Benjamin. Consider this your home. Your home, do you hear?"

I couldn't believe how effortless it was, how surreal, the luck that had found me. It would have been foolish to refuse, ungrateful to decline. I was a curious child with dreams, and the man before me knew I was that sort of child. The meeting of the dreamer and the granter of dreams.

3

MY YOUNGER BROTHER OMAR was afraid of the water. He didn't know how to swim and he was ashamed of that fact, afraid to be teased. It was indeed laughable because everyone knew how to swim. It was absurd not to know how to swim growing up in the islands. But he did not venture into the sea alone.

Here is my brother walking down the dusty road wearing a plain white shirt and cargo pants, smoking a Philip Morris. It is a brisk evening like the evenings of those other years when he was a child of the town that had been his entire life, all twenty-eight years, a mélange of devotion and rancor and monotony. But he loves San Jacinto. Certainly, he loves home. He walks past the line of tall palm trees, past the dim-lighted houses. He heeds everything around him like a prying stranger arriving at a place for the first time. But he knows this road, even if darkness obscures its edges and bends.

Omar does not look back, does not flinch for a moment. He passes by a group of people and does not look at them. He lowers his cap and gazes at the ground as he overhears them talk about a fiesta in another barrio. He is acquainted with the conversation, he knows how it runs. He could have joined the crowd. He could have made puns and gone along with the banter. But words do not appeal to him any longer; life is all unending chatter. He prefers reticence if not solitude.

He ambles alone in the dark. He kicks the dirt. He used to do this as a child, walking barefoot from place to place. He finds comfort in the dust on his feet, the dust that speaks of earth, the earth where everything rots and flourishes. Memories scatter here and there, the ones he always held on to because he thought they would someday save him. For instance, the glow of the fields on summer nights as though the glint of scattered light in the sky reflected on the land. As moonbeams fell, stillness leaked everywhere, passing through the frail branches of trees and reaching even the hardened hearts of men. Then music came after, not in the expected way that one hears it, but something more divine, like symphonic sounds of glory bursting through the sky. This was the happiness he knew, the tranquility of the evening, of his loved ones sleeping soundly near him. A simple life was what he truly desired.

He takes a large puff of smoke and blows a ring, and then another, and watches the ring dissolve into a mass of cloud. This is the last cigarette of his life. He thinks of no one now, not our dead mother whom he never knew, whose grave he visited alone once a year since he turned eleven, bringing with him what he had been told were her favorite flowers, chrysanthemums, imagining what she was like, telling her the intimate particulars of his thoughts that he did not share with anyone. He used to think that his wayward life was mainly the result of the absence of a mother and a woman's intuitive and sensible ways. He wanted to understand why he lived and she did not. He found this to be ill-conceived by the god who let this happen, a tragedy, for he found living unbearable and thus felt undeserving of the life bestowed on him. He did not think of our dead father, especially not the tumultuous years nor the tragic sound of his soul collapsing. He did not think of me, the brother with fatuous dreams who ran off to America. He did not think of the harsh details of life that bring about a man's demise nor did he ponder on the God who has let him down. It is of no use now, this endless, pointless questioning, the mad desire to understand and the dejection of not arriving at any clarity. This was the crux of his life and it had taken him to where he is now, on a solitary walk to the sea where freedom awaits him.

He looks at the brilliant sky with its gleam of stars. For a moment he concedes that wonder abounds. For once, he feels less lonely.

But he decides it is too late to love this world, it is too much for him.

This is the only way, he thinks, as he feels the white sand under his feet, the water just a few steps away. He surveys the sea, the fears he had of it since he was a child now mysteriously dispelled, and in its place, a resolute embracing. He observes the world unfold before him. The faint but steady light on the far horizon, the hum of the sea, the rising tide, the full moon holding the world together. He revels at this final image. He remembers a folktale told to him as a child, of the sea goddess, Magwayen. He offers her a short prayer. Omar takes his first step into the sea. And here is my pious brother praying before his most un-Catholic act.

But these are just my own reveries, my fabrications of that evening when my brother walked away from home, never to be heard from again. All I have of him are his ashes that sit next to Jose Rizal's book *Noli Me Tangere*. Touch Me Not. Whoever touched Omar reduced him to ashes. He is now a sentiment, a melancholy word, an ache in my heart.

This is how I've been spending this day, inside my head, sifting the memories as they come. There is a lot to retrieve—faith, stories, scattered laughter in the sunbeams. Also—regrets, grinding undertones, curses in the night. It seems that there is a door whose knob I once turned to enter, and I lingered inside, the boy that I was in those discarded years. And when I rushed for the exit and closed the door behind me, it became shut forever, inaccessible except to dubious memory. As a boy, I was nostalgic about the possibilities. There was something seductive about the future, my mind's play of dreams oblivious of impediments. But now it is the past that consumes me the most.

Of course they leave me all this mess because I am the one with the job and the promising future and strength of character. Because I allegedly have my life together. Because I have been turned into an abstraction. I am Benjamin Aragon from San Jacinto, a poor small, town unknown to the rest of the world. I went above and beyond. And yet. Anywhere I turn, I see my brother, I cannot shake him off. And this is where all my mad ravings begin when a crackle from the other world shifts to familiar intonations.

"Benjamin!" I hear Omar calling out my name, his voice on the verge of crying. He is fretful, when being left alone for a moment seems like an act of betrayal.

"Over here! Look up, I'm on top of the tree," I yell at him from above, staring down at his three-year old eyes now wide with relief as he hears my voice.

I want to be a child again of those years, of that guiltless time. *"Catch me if you can!"* he dares me, my young restless brother, running off into the fields leaving behind a trail of dust. We had each other all day, every day, catching grasshoppers and butterflies and giving them names. We climbed trees, collected spiders and put them on a coconut palm midrib to let them fight.

Leaf. Shoe. Mango. He named a thing that best resembled the shape of a cloud in the sky. Omar was a child of extremes. He said the saddest things or the silliest. One minute he was screaming and the next he was silent. He could be unruly all morning and then later sulk in a corner. Sulking as if he was so completely offended by something that he wouldn't tell you what it was. There was a kind of sensitivity to his silence that gnawed at you.

I fancy that he is around, watching me, which I do not mind. I would like a moment with my brother, man to man, even if he is enraged, his back turned against me. I would like to tell him a story, have many drinks and pass out in oblivion. Or take a walk in the dead of night. Anything for our last words. But mostly, I would just like to listen to him.

Omar had beautiful eyes. For me to have understood what happened to my brother during all those years, I should have looked at his eyes. Had I looked into them long enough, I would have seen that those eyes were laden with anguish, they pleaded for mercy. For at times you chance upon a malevolent world, and you realize that you are completely alone, there is no one to turn to but yourself. No one really knows us. We may all hold hands, share wonders and laments, but we are like boats anchored waiting for the night to pass. We simply occupy, side by side, a space to grieve on the rough seas or delight in its quietude together. But in the morning, we all depart and become solitary. Life is lonely this way sometimes, and perhaps my brother lived his years with this kind of loneliness. And when I walk on the ground where our old hut sits, the earth fades to other meanings and I become a prodigal walking in a strange place. Here in the land of my beginnings, the past is not a happy place to revisit. I am disturbing the dead. And just this once, for Omar's sake, I say a prayer to appease my brother. So I close my eyes and picture his eight-year old face in solemn prayer. I attempt to exclaim hosannas to an absent god. I wait for the tranquility that my brother felt when he closed his eyes and communed with his God. I wait for the kind of peace that descends when one prays. I empty myself and wait.

4

IT IS THE FIRST OF JUNE, my second day in San Jacinto. It is
the beginning of the wet season and already it is a somber
day, as it should be, for the occasion of my homecoming is
not a joyous one. Mild rain fell past eleven last night and
strong winds howled like a wild animal. It went on for hours.
I curled up in bed and faced the large window. In the darkness
of my room, light from the deserted street pierced through the
thin drapes. I imagined the chaos outside. Leaves trembling,
twigs falling, dust spinning, everything amok. That was what
I wanted, a cast of the world's momentary rage. I felt the soft-
ness of my bed, the bed of someone who was at once myself
and someone else. Who was that distinct other, that version
of myself that tossed and turned and withered as the night
deepened? Then the faint light that settled on the drapes faded
into shadows, shadows of selves that pulsated, throbbed like
a provoked heart. And then something else pervaded in the
stillness right before slumber set in; an unsettling weight, a
sally of portents, the world skipping a beat. A swirl of inner
tumult passed. I lay on my back and covered my eyes with a
pillow and fell asleep.

The morning-after, this dawn of ashen tint, it is still a
drowsy world. There is no inkling of commotion; people are
still basking in their sleep. There are branches and litter and

toppled pots. I would like to find comfort this way, to stand here like this and just be present in the moment, to take in the early morning sky, standing like another ordinary mortal, nothing to be intense about, joining the world in its transitions from night to day, sleep to waking, witnessing the little details of life unfold, smelling the flavor of the air infused with earth and water, sipping coffee from a large mug, still, whole, combing for other signs of life apart from my own beating heart. But only for a moment. In the last few hours I have plunged into the lowest depths of misery. And a dream last night led me to a time long past, to a displaced region in the mind where one's memory is summoned to bear witness to an occasion. In the dream, I lay motionless on the floor of my father's room. It was a balmy evening, nothing stirred. Suddenly I shouted so forcefully that the sugar canes lurched as if a violent wind advanced from the farthest ends of the fields. It seemed like a storm rose from the depths and it remained that way for a while, my voice and the storm making a raging noise until I woke up on my bed with the sheets in disarray and my forehead moist with sweat. But I let that dream suspend for a little while for indeed I am aggrieved, haunted by ghosts and furious at each one of them. I catch myself listening intently to the rise and fall of their voices inside my head, each wanting to be heard. I am the fraying pieces of a man in grief and I am beset with guilt and shame and ire.

So I load a teaspoon of sugar into my coffee as I think of the thick smoke coming out of San Jacinto's sugar mill and the air smells of molasses. I pace back and forth, pensive in the dawn light as I await news of Don Rafael's real plight. Better alive than dead. I would like to gather my thoughts and assemble them before he feels my outrage.

5

THE TRAVEL TIME from Los Angeles to Sugbu city is fifteen hours. I arrived at Sugbu in the evening and spent the night at a nearby motel. I rented a car and left for San Jacinto yesterday morning. The three-hour drive was pleasant. There weren't many cars yet and the road had new asphalt. There were the usual overloaded buses with adults and children sitting on the roof holding on to their belongings. I rolled down the windows to catch a whiff of salty air. After about two hours of driving, I pulled over along a small stretch of beach, and for a while just sat inside the car. Something about the movement of the sea made me linger there, listening to the murmur of the currents breeze into life. And the sea was mysterious, commanding, as though it was not simply a body of water but a keeper of all things consummate and tragic. I longed for my brother in between the movement and stillness of the water, and then it occurred to me that I lost him many, many years ago, long before I came home to collect his ashes. It appealed to me to watch a group of children make creaking sounds. A young girl collected sea shells, and another dipped her sand-filled feet into the water. A pair of young lovers held hands along the shore under the romance of a cobalt sky. The woman burst into giggles when the man whispered something in her ear, words of endearment, perhaps. I sat there like an old man lost in heavy meandering thought, waiting for the hours to pass, in resignation that what was left of my life were musings, indifference, and the long silences between idle hours. Somehow, I missed my own youth. I was always older than my age, always at once both adult and child, always looking out for the family. I think I am losing my mind.

Speaking of lovers, I have to call Cora. I promised to let her know of my plight once I arrived here in San Jacinto. *I am doing very poorly, my dear Cora, if you must know.*

That windless summer day when I first met her remains lodged in my memory. That afternoon, she shrugged her shoulders and flashed her first stroke of indifference at me, the artless man, who combed for words to say to her. I don't know the artistry of making a good first impression on a woman; I leave it to others to carry out such affectations. My first encounter with her was unoriginal. I simply handed her the earring she had dropped on the floor. I don't recall now what I said to her exactly, as I have lost track of my numerous blunders. I felt inept standing beside a fetching, beautiful woman who seemed to be in command of her world. I felt like an idiot. I was about to mumble an excuse to leave, when she smiled and said, "So your shirt speaks a lot about you?" *What? What?* I said, nervous and pleased that she had not yet fled to the nearby store to get rid of me. "Your shirt." She meant the black shirt I wore that had the words "Bullshittal Lobe" above a drawing of a human brain with diagrams of which areas concentrate on the various types of bullshit known to man. How odd the random things which redeem one. So it was in the emptiness of a summer afternoon that we met, as people do, in the most ordinary of situations. We keep each other company. In the beginning we fucked mostly out of loneliness, the rest for convenience. Over time our relations evolved but we do not talk about it. That we are very close is one way of putting it. One night I rehearsed in my head a few times what I was to say to her if we ever had that conversation. I wrote it all down on a piece of torn paper. Then I read it out aloud a few times, pacing back and forth in my living room. Then I took a walk around my neighborhood and practiced reading what I wrote, with feeling and appropriate pauses and the right modulation of voice. I got a few startled looks from those who caught me talking to myself. When I got home I drank a few beers. And then a few more. Maudlin and feeling brave, I felt ready to give Cora my whole speech, so I called her with the intention of asking her to meet me somewhere the following day, ideally a quiet place, something romantic even, like a park with giant trees whose thick canopies catch the sunlight, or even a walk on a small hidden street lined with assorted flowers that I could pluck and give to her. That was, and still is to this day, the extent of my imagination when exploring my romantic side. But then some stupid, inconsequential remarks kept coming out of my mouth instead. I tried to tell her. I tried but I failed.

She sketches. Some mornings when I wake up, I find her sitting on the stairs leading to the back porch drawing on a sketch pad. Good morning, Cora, I say to her. She raises her left arm and waves her hand without looking at me and continues to sketch. There are things that can be drawn from this, from the way she sits alone on the stairs not wanting to be bothered with anything, especially not with men and their hurried goodbyes. You can know a woman this way, in her moments of quiet, in the way she looks at the sky with eyes that have taken more depth before she begins to bow her head and resume her drawing. And so in these precise moments of what I call her fragility, when she seems to be immersed in deep thought, creative, I make her a cappuccino or some cocktail depending on the time of day, and play the mellow playlist on her iPod as background music to show her that I do have, you know, a sensitive side? I do. But she does not hear. I often wonder what she thinks about when she does those drawings. I fancy that they are radiant or nostalgic or melancholy thoughts. Something about vistas and the music of rain, and perhaps, the faintness of hearts. Once, in the earlier days of our closeness, she cried quietly in my arms. I do not know who she shed those tears for. I felt oddly special that she turned to me for comfort, if holding her like that was a comfort to her.

Like me, no stranger to poverty and the desire to get out of it, she also hails from the northern part of Sugbu, a town called Castro. By this alone we formed an immediate bond. It seemed as though we had known each other for a long time, like we shared a common past, the same northern history, the same kind of poverty. When her father passed away when she was nine, she was sent off to live with an alcoholic uncle. She ran away from there and for quite some time no one knew what had become of her. After many years, she reappeared bearing gifts for her ailing mother and four siblings. There is a period in her disappearance from her family that remains vague and mysterious, but I do not interrogate her about this, though at times when I sense that she is sad, it makes me wonder if it had to do with what happened to her in all those unaccounted-for years. What is known is that eventually she settled in Los Angeles after she got married to her pen pal, Ian Thomas, a white man of European descent, twenty-one years her senior. He was good to her, taught her about the ways of the world, embraced her culture fully. He understood that she had to support her family by sending them money every month. With him she experienced what it was like to have a stable, peaceful life. But tragedy struck when he was killed in a crash while riding his motorcycle. He died instantly. She was supposed to go with him on that ride, but she begged off at the last minute due to a migraine. That day she wished she had died with him, for she thought that she could no longer face a life of despair. And yet. Given to superstitions and belief in fate, she reasoned that perhaps it was not yet her time to die, that there must be some other purpose to her living. A little over a year after Ian's death, she went to nursing school and got herself a license as a registered nurse. She is a survivor, and beautiful, as all scarred women are, sailing courageously through the murky waters of a life.

Corazon! I say to her when I am in a serious mood, and she rolls her eyes when I call her that. It is, after all, her real name, and aptly so, for her heart is full of compassion. Her tough exterior does not fool me. She can put up a wall as high as she wants yet I know it is all a façade. She works at a nursing home in a sketchy part of Los Angeles. I suggested she find work in a safer area. But danger did not matter to her. She loves her patients, she said, and has adjusted well to the place. Many times she has come to me bringing her sadness over a patient's death.

"Remember Joan, the patient in room 104? I've told you about her a while back."

"What about her?"

"We were out in the patio smoking. We talked, like we always do. Then she said she won't be going out on the patio anymore, that she is tired. I didn't believe her because she seemed fine, and she never missed a day being outside smoking or not. Anyway, that afternoon, she talked a lot about her son, how proud she was of him. But he rarely visited her, and he's local. I do not think it's right that he hardly comes to see her but of course I did not tell her that. So that was all Joan talked about, her son. The next day, she passed away. Just like that. I couldn't believe it. It still spooks me to this day. It was almost like she knew death was coming. You know what her last words were to me?

"What?"

"'I love my son very much.' And when the son came to pick up Joan's belongings, I mentioned it to him. I told him that his mother's last words to me were that she loved him very much. And tears fell from his eyes as he went through photos of both of them in an old album that she kept in her drawer. And I started to cry too. And we just stood there quietly wiping the tears from our eyes. You know there are days when I can't stand this job. I get too attached to the patients."

"Because you care, you have a good heart. Others don't. You've seen it."

"It is a lonely life, isn't it? I do not want to die in a facility. When I am old and useless, I want to go home and tend a garden. Or raise chickens. Have a piggery. You know how I want to die, Benjamin?"

"How?"

"Looking at the sky, in the land of my birth."

"Do we have to be this dramatic? We're fairly young to think of morbid thoughts like that."

"These things do not cross your mind, considering that we deal with mortality quite often? Besides you never know when your time will come. Any day could be your last day. Think about it."

She was the first person I phoned when I learned of Omar's death. I was on the road, she was at work. I called her five times but didn't leave a voice mail. When I arrived home, I sent her a text message *My brother is dead* then I turned off my phone, lay down on the sofa and stared at the ceiling for hours. I was in shock. She called me back that evening. "I am so sorry. How are you holding up?" What was I meant to say to her? That I have turned slightly mad in the world of the bereaved? I was about to step out for a long walk but suddenly lost the will to do so. I longed to curl up on the sofa, switch off the lights and cower in the dark. I caught a glimpse of the bible at the bottom of my bookshelf and realized it was Sunday. I used to hear Mass regularly on Sundays until it got in the way of work and sleep and mundane chores. I am an infidel. Dear God, you are cruel. You are a fucking joke.

"Benjamin? Are you there? Do you need anything?"

I suppose I am entitled to a bit of indulging, such is the business of bereavement. This was my moment to be catered to for anything. But what does one really need but decent sleep, and, yes, the occasional lapses of wanting the dead to come back to life.

"Yes, I am here. I'm okay, I guess. I don't know. I'll be fine," I said, trying to sound unshaken but I knew my voice fell flat. I couldn't tell her that I was a shambles. But what did it matter? Did I fear she might find it unmanly? I walked out the door and sat on the front steps and smoked. Cigarette butts were behind the bushes, an unsightly mess I had made since I had taken to smoking.

"You have been drinking, haven't you?"

Yes, Cora, I have been drinking. I am, after all, my father's son. And yes, Cora, after making love to you, when you are sound asleep, I do watch you, your curled shape traced by the moon, and then my heart grows heavy. One of these days, I will only hold you and not speak of anything at all. "Cry," she once advised me. I did not, like most men who leave such an undertaking to women. *I cope differently,* I said. It was partially true. I have cried before, but never in front of anyone.

"Only a few beers, sweetie, that's all. Nothing to be concerned about. And I'm not going to drive, I promise you." Also, a few shots of gin and tonic. And a bottle of vodka was waiting to be opened. I lied. I lie, if only to appease matters. She remained quiet on the other line as I tried to make sense of her silence. I knew she was skeptical. My drinking (when it's more than three shots of any liquor) often bothers her. My inattentiveness bothers her. My inarticulateness. The list goes on, no doubt.

We have our moments, Cora and I, prattle and sense, hoot and rest, mild derisions, long silences. And always, she remains the woman at whose beck my world staggers in all directions towards, then takes me at last to a lofty height. Someday I will confess to her the insoluble musings of a man who has ever loved a woman.

6

I HAD JUST MADE IT to the town square and was about to
make a right turn on the corner of the Alejandro pharmacy
when my rental car got a flat tire. That should have been my
forewarning that my day was not going to go well, yet I felt
lucky that there was an auto shop nearby. I was told by a young
fellow that the owner had stepped out so I had to wait until he
got back. I preferred to take a stroll instead of sitting on the
bench waiting. The car stalled just a few feet from the shop,
so I told him that they could go ahead and change the tires in
case I had not come back by the time the owner returned. I
left him the car keys and went for a walk.

Walking along, there must be something, I thought, that
would draw me back to San Jacinto's quiet allure, to its old
beauty. Something, even a cliché, like recalling an old flame
and remembering the reasons why you loved her. I expected
a few turns of nostalgia. For instance, the row of Narra trees
behind the church where I took shade and observed the
crowd, or the eaves of the old municipal hall where I stood
for hours seeking cover from the rain. I thought, when a pair
of kids laughing caught my attention, that I would immediately
declare: *Ah, yes, of course! We too laughed, my brother and I, over
there by the garden of azaleas and yellow roses, where you kids are
standing looking at the sky and deciphering those strange-looking*

clouds. A few nostalgic moments did emerge, familiar structures and recognizable sounds but that was all. That I felt that way, bereft of a particular feeling, left me unsettled, even a little ashamed of myself. What had I become? I willed myself to feel what one was supposed to feel about a homecoming, the gladness, the comfort of familiar things, the cherished bygones. Nothing of those feelings came to me until the heat of the sun made me tired and I stopped to rest on a bench under an acacia tree. From where I sat I could see the old wooden bridge that led to the sugar mill. Immediately what came into my mind was one morning when Omar and I had stood on the bridge and threw stones into the muddy water. We challenged each other as to who could throw the stones the furthest, and whoever lost would have to carry the other on his back walking from the town square towards home. We did silly things like that to amuse ourselves. We talked walking all the way to the bridge. Our sentences began with the words *It would be cool.* It would be cool if we had super powers. It would be cool if we could fly or be invisible. It would be cool if we had bikes. It would be cool if we had lots and lots of money. We picked up stones along the way. What a hot day it was, everything was gilded with sunlight. "Are you ready?" Omar asked. "You go first," I said. We agreed to do it five times, and every single time, he threw it further than I did. I smiled as I remembered his chuckle when he beat me, the way he jumped so high in utter joy at his small victory. I do not know what it was about that memory that made me suddenly grow weak, like something had hit me in the head, or in the heart, those fragile spots that make us vulnerable. So all was not lost after all, my affections for my town were still there, perhaps not love, but something else that I had yet to name. I sat on the bench for a while, thinking how distant those days were but how real it seemed when I remembered them, as if I heard my own voice telling Omar that he was now too big and heavy for me to carry him on my back and that I had to put him down before we reached home.

At a whim, I hailed a tricycle to take me around town.

The tricycle can accommodate five people of average weight, four on the sidecar and one behind the driver. I sat on the sidecar's second row. The woman sitting in front of me was old and frail. I knew she was on her way to church because she held a rosary in her hand. During the ride, I imagined her hearing Mass and paying careful attention to the priest. After Mass, she would light a candle and recite all the names of the dead and pray that their souls were in heaven. I imagined too that she would kneel as she said the novena or recited all the mysteries of the holy rosary. And after all these, she would touch, one by one, the statues of the saints, say a prayer at each stop, and touch the statues once more before she left. I wanted to ask her to say a prayer for me, a request that she would find bizarre. For why could I not do it myself? Go inside the church and say a prayer. How difficult was that? Very difficult, given my present predicament. I looked at her and couldn't help but ponder the wisdom of old age. I thought how she must have lived all her life in San Jacinto. I caught a glimpse of her old, wrinkled hands. They were hands that had given so much to this world. Giving without taking. Giving without questioning. Giving with a heart that endures. She disembarked quietly from the tricycle. She walked towards the church until she joined the crowd and disappeared before my eyes. Bless you, I said to her in my mind.

I was the only passenger left. On impulse, I asked the young driver how much he earned in one day. I offered to pay him triple if he didn't take on any more passengers and just took me around for a couple of hours. His eyes widened, and he said, "Anywhere you want, sir. For what you offered to pay me, I can take you around all day until you get tired." I was surprised at how he called me sir. Was I that set apart from the rest? Was it my clean fingernails, my Hugo Boss cologne, my Gap jeans? My brand-new Nikes? My I Love Los Angeles shirt? That is not even true. I do not love Los Angeles, but I do not hate it either.

"Where do you want to go, sir? To the beach?"

"Where do you suggest I go?" I asked back.

"Well, if you do not have any place in mind, then I'd say the beach. There is a new resort, The Sands. You should check it out, sir. Very nice. A lot of pretty ladies."

I acquiesced and told him to stop calling me sir. I did not yet reveal that I was a local too, just like him. At a guess he seemed to be about eighteen. Had I not left this town, I could have been a tricycle driver just like him. At eighteen I lived in Sugbu city and went to the university to get a degree in occupational therapy. While studying, I worked part-time as a janitor at a local hospital for about a year. Then I worked as a clerk for Don Rafael's cargo forwarding business until I finished my studies. I did not, like most youths in the city, go to clubs or indulge in drinking or drugs. Most thought of me as a weird fellow, a nerd. I was looked down as a *probinsi-yano*, a man from the province, therefore awkward in speech and social skills, and ignorant of the ways of urban life. They didn't make fun of me but I was not invited to their social functions. I was not part of the popular crowd. My clothes were ordinary, plain shirts and brandless pants, a pair of worn out sneakers that I didn't throw away until the soles finally fell apart. My classmates wore clothing with brand labels you wouldn't miss. I took the jeepney every day. Sometimes Don Rafael gave me a lift if he was going in my direction. I always asked to be dropped off a block or two from the university as I did not wish to be seen coming out of a Mercedes Benz. I did not care about making a good impression on everyone except my teachers whom I considered important figures who would direct me to a bright future. I did exceptionally well in all my classes. What I lacked in fashion sense and social finesse, I compensated by being top of my class. Every semester I was on the dean's list. I had no grievances of any sort as my life was going in the manner I had envisioned it would. I was enrolled at the university, had a small income from my part-time job, lived in Don Rafael's comfortable house and I was not asked to pay rent nor make monetary contributions toward utility bills. Does it sound strange, that back then, I always knew I was going to attain some level of success, moderate, perhaps, but success nonetheless? And where were Omar and papa amid all of this? They were in the far future I conjured in my head, a pleasant April evening, papa wearing a crisp polo shirt standing next to Omar who is browsing through books inside the house that I will, someday, build for the three of us.

I welcomed the young driver's suggestion that we go to the beach. I didn't care for the resort or how fancy it was, and I certainly was not interested in the pretty ladies. I longed to be near the sea of my childhood. There were times when I was young that I felt deprived of the elation of being near the sea because Omar did not get any pleasure from it, and I felt that the right thing to do was show solidarity with him rather than pursue my own gratification.

"I have to get gas," the young driver said while making a turn for the Shell station.

"Sure. Here take this money and fill up your tank."

"Thank you, sir. Thank you very much."

"What is your name?" I asked.

"Ricardo. But they call me Rico," he said and took the money from my hand.

I looked around and headed for a *sari-sari* store to get some liquor and snacks. I purchased my supplies without a fuss and headed back to where Rico waited for me.

Off we went cruising through our beloved town. Carpe diem, they say.

When we reached *barangay* Kawit, the sea was visible and within reach. Had I instructed Rico to stop and park the tricycle on the side of the road, we just had to walk about forty feet before we would be walking on the sand. He drove slowly because the potholed road was narrow and crowded with pedestrians who crossed without looking for oncoming vehicles. I relished the sea from my seat. The water shimmered under the sunlight. I was reminded of the time when papa taught me how to swim because it was a day just like that, a day so flooded by the fierce northern light that it was impossible not to bask in that sunshine, impossible to sulk indoors and feel sorry for yourself. The water was clear and calm as usual. Papa simply held my chin while I paddled and then he let go and I was left there paddling and kicking my legs, struggling not to sink. He was nearby, ready to grab me whenever the water rose slightly above my mouth. He did it repeatedly, holding my chin and letting go, and every time it seemed like I was about to sink, I forged a scenario in my head, that I was there alone with no one to save me, that I had to stay afloat in order to live, I had to swim or die, and as I was having those thoughts, it turned out that I swam effortlessly and headed back to shallow water. The memory of that day was prominent in my head as Rico tried to maneuver his tricycle into the pedestrian-filled street. I imagined schools of tiny fish and sea weed visible under the clear water. The waves gently lapped. What I saw while sitting inside the tricycle—children frolicking in the peaceful water, *bangkas* anchored in the shore, the commotion of the nearby wet market—solidified the feeling of being home. My sea, my sea, I cried in my head.

7

AS A CHILD I THOUGHT I WAS BORN in the wrong part of the world. My curiosity, my restless nature had no place in San Jacinto. Living the way we lived all those trying years, I learned to seek out other places in my mind. There must be, I imagined, something more exciting than waking up to that endless verdure, to the same section of sky and its predictable blue variations; there must be something less dull than waiting for harvest season and praying for good weather; something more engaging, more promising. And so there were times in the stormy months when I fell into a bit of a trance, looking out into the expanse, gazing at the sky that seemed to announce rain and the nimbus clouds assembled without end, that I was transported to unheard-of places. In my inner world, I lived outside the confines of poverty. I was a man with a respectable name navigating the bright boulevard of a foreign city somewhere. At other times I was standing on a pier mesmerized by seagulls, and down the street, flares of light fell on the windows of shops selling trinkets of gold and emerald green. What an assortment of magical worlds I conjured up in my head, sitting there by the propped-up window of our tiny hut, drifting, my beloved San Jacinto fading before my eyes.

On Saturday mornings I made a point to go to St. Ignatius church to attend catechism and take advantage of the free books of all sorts that were handed out, not just the bible. Some were picture books and most were old editions of school books that had been phased out. I was once reprimanded for taking three books, as I was not aware of the 'One book per person' policy. Since I was the only boy my age who went there consistently, the lady in charge began to recognize me and stopped minding that I took more than one book at a time. Her name was Soledad Gutierrez, a volunteer from a remote barrio in the faraway island of Miramar. When she was four, her parents were accidentally killed when a gunfight ensued between the New People's Army and the local police. A religious congregation took her in and cared for her. She didn't know what had become of her younger brother. She told me this story over lunch one day when she brought me a boiled egg and a peanut butter sandwich, an act of kindness from a stranger that I will never forget. It was the first time I had tasted peanut butter and I found it so special that I only ate half of the sandwich and saved the rest for Omar. Next time I will bring an extra sandwich for your brother, she said. I remember that her long hair, parted in the middle, went down to her waist. She looked so pristine sitting on the bench under the coconut trees, and so collected, as though when she told me about her family, it was not her own childhood tragedy she was narrating but simply an ordinary account of someone else's life. Miss G, as everyone called her, stayed an extra hour to teach me, her most eager and clever pupil she said, how to write and read, and how to do basic mathematics. She taught me folklore, too, like the legend of Maria Makiling, a spirit and guardian of the mountains. Maria Makiling sometimes disguised herself as a peasant girl to help the poor. She rewarded the good-hearted ones and punished the wicked.

I was overcome with emotion every Saturday when I was with Miss G because she was compassionate and gentle, she challenged me to think and encouraged me to ask questions without fear of being chided.

"Does God answer prayers, Miss G?"

"Yes".

"As in, immediately?"

"Sometimes. But the trick is to pay attention because if you don't, you're gonna miss the answer. And bear in mind that no is an answer too."

"You mean God doesn't grant all your wishes even if you prayed so hard for them?"

"No, if it's not in His divine plan."

"Divine plan? What is that?"

"Have faith, Benjamin, in yourself, above all."

"Miss G?"

"Yes, Benjamin?"

"Can we talk about the stars next time?"

"If you do your homework".

My sort of unconventional schooling with her lasted for a year. Omar rarely come along with me those early Saturday mornings as he preferred to sleep. I shared with him what I learned that morning or about my conversations with Miss G, and depending on his mood, he was eager to hear them or went about his own way. One Saturday Miss G didn't show up, and the next, and then not at all anymore, and each night for about a month after she stopped coming to San Jacinto, she was in my prayers. God, I pray that Miss G comes back. God, please watch over Miss G. God, I miss Miss G. God, where is Miss G?

Like all other families in town, we were Catholics and we took it seriously. We went to church every Sunday and all

Catholic holidays of obligation. Papa was big on God. He used
to say, "God will be angry if you do that." Or, "Just pray to God
and everything will be fine." We used to pray a lot, the three
of us together, papa and Omar and I. We said prayers before
and after meals, before going to bed, before taking a shower,
before doing anything. It wasn't papa who started the practice.
It was his father, and his father's father. It was the doing of all
fathers and mothers of centuries ago who bore children. It was
the Spaniards who first introduced Christianity to the islands.
When Ferdinand Magellan arrived in Sugbu and met the chief-
tain Datu Humabon, Magellan preached about the greatness
of Christianity. Then the natives believed and converted, and
Datu Humabon was baptized and renamed Carlos, in honor
of the Spanish king, Charles I. Magellan erected a large cross
to mark the baptismal site, and gave Juana, Humabon's wife,
an image of the baby Jesus as a gift. The cross still stands today,
a landmark frequented by tourists. Since then Christianity
became a way of life, more like a list of things that one ought to
become. And thou shall not do this, and thou shall not do that.
And I have yet to see the point of all these, the righteousness
and guilt and all the suffering.

"God will reward you in heaven." *Why in heaven?* I asked
as a child. But I was told not to ask questions like that as it
denoted doubt. One was supposed to have absolute faith only.
Omar was especially religious. He always volunteered to lead
the prayers if papa was not around. He knelt and put his palms
together and closed his eyes like a good Catholic boy. I went
along, bored through all the mysteries of the rosary. Sometimes I giggled when I forgot the words to a prayer and he
would give me a sideways glance of disapproval. As if I were
irreverent, as if I just committed a sin. And so I became quiet

and let him recite the rest. Then there is always the pause. There is that quiet moment when you bow your head and speak to God about your personal intentions. And here my mind drifted to other things, like what are the chances of me going to school or how many stars there are in the sky. Meanwhile, Omar remained in his pious zone. What was he reflecting about? What do you ask from God when you are six? A toy, I suppose, or a hearty breakfast, for a change.

Home to us was a *nipa* hut divided into two main sections, the living room and the kitchen. Omar and I slept on the living room floor. Papa slept in the kitchen area. A thin curtain separated his sleeping corner from where the cooking and washing of dishes were done. There was no toilet or shower. There was a backdoor from the kitchen that led to a small plot of garden. The garden was tended by mama when she was still alive. She planted bamboos, a variety of blooms, *malunggay*, tomatoes, banana. The three of us took turns watering the plants. The hut was about twelve feet from the main road. To our left and right were sugarcane plantations. We walked to the well to get water. It was a twenty-minute walk one way. The well was out in the open behind an abandoned, dilapidated cottage and Omar and I took our showers by the well. On Sundays when we heard Mass, Omar loved to wear his favorite shirt, the one with the faded Voltes V logo on it. Omar liked sitting on the front pew when we went to hear Mass. And this used to annoy me, the way he didn't want to sit at the back close to the exit doors. He said he wanted a clear view of the altar and a good look at Padre Carlos, the parish priest, who had an expressionless face and high-pitched voice. Omar sat there with his hands on his lap, the right over the left, feet together, his back straight, not once turning his head sideways.

He listened attentively to Father Ramon's sermon. On three occasions, we have witnessed Father Ramon admonish two churchgoers for talking to each other while he was giving his sermon. The first time I witnessed it, I was shocked to see Padre Ramon so annoyed to the point of interrupting his own sermon and embarrassing the churchgoers. Often, I sat there with my mind elsewhere, the sermon about the gospel of Mark or John turned into another noise, like the noise of vendors outside the church begging for attention. I was drifting, I suppose, as I still do now.

When Mass was over, the adults went to the *carenderia* to drink palm wine or cerveza. We children wandered about the plaza. It had a playground with wide marble benches on all corners and a garden of azaleas. There were vendors selling cotton candy and balloons and plastic toys. If we weren't playing tag or hide and seek, we just sat on the grass and looked at passersby.

Those were our best years, in a way, because we were happy, our joys were pure. Nobody harmed us. We were free to wander about. There was no fear about getting abducted or lost. We always found our way no matter how far we ventured, no matter how dark the night had turned, and perhaps this was from instinct or perhaps because we knew our land because we were its children. Townsfolk always knew who your parents or relatives were so there was no reason for concern if indeed one got lost for you were offered shelter or guided back home. All that we knew was the life we had—ordinary, yes, and pitiful too, but there was no other way to live it. In summer time, the children of *haciendros* drove by the town plaza on their way to their beach resorts. Sometimes they stopped at the *sari-sari* store and bought anything they wanted. They hung out there with their car doors wide open and the radio blasting out music. They were always given the benches to sit on, and were attended to with special hospitality. We looked at them in awe like they were little gods. They had their chauffeurs and maids attending to their every whim. They were boisterous, and they came down to San Jacinto for a holiday or to attend the annual town fiesta. Watching those illustrious kids made me realize how set apart we were from them. When their cars drove by, I said to myself that someday, someday, I too would be driving my own car and would speed away without a care in the world. There, on the occasions of my momentary drifting, I rolled out my dreams and said to myself that I must convince papa to let me work at the farm. Even then I was already determined to raise our station in life. These musings about my fanciful future were often disrupted when Omar called out my name and placed my hand on his growling stomach. His hunger had to wait for a while, as I had to check on *Manang* Fidela's mood. She owned a *carenderia* and *sari-sari* store and opened credit for everyone. But if you owed more than eighty pesos, you could no longer buy anything unless you paid the full amount. There were times when she turned us down and said that papa needed to pay at least half of what was owed before she would allow us to buy anything. Twice I stole from her store. On these two occasions, there was no customer and she was nowhere in sight. On the first time, I waited for her and was keen to beg for more credit but when I turned to look at Omar waiting outside, I could tell from his expression that he was famished. I went outside to the back of the store and saw that *Manang* Fidela was speaking to someone. I went back inside and took biscuits and put them inside my pocket. I then grabbed a can of sardines and left the store hurriedly and motioned Omar to follow me. When I stole the second time, it was a deliberate act, I am ashamed to admit. I went there with the intention to steal and took a few packs of assorted biscuits, a can of sardines, a can of corned beef, and candies. That night, I felt so guilty that I prayed the Joyful, Sorrowful, and Glorious mysteries of the holy rosary and promised God that I would never do it again. I did not tell Omar and certainly not papa as he would have punished me. I did not steal again after that; my conscience couldn't bear it. I had to resort to antics and storytelling to keep Omar amused when he was starving, to make him forget the hunger and waiting and despair. But to be fair with *Manang* Fidela, there were other times when she took pity on us and gave us bread and fried bananas and Coke for free. If she was in an especially pleasant mood, she would also give us chocolates or marbles. She never married nor had children. The rumor was that she turned bitter because of a broken promise. I overheard this information from a customer who made a remark about how particularly ill-tempered *Manang* Fidela was that afternoon. "She's in her spinster mood." "The man she loved left town and promised to return for her but never did." "No wonder she's always crabby." I couldn't forget that one morning she said to me, in a low voice, as if almost embarrassed, "You're Aurora's son, aren't you? I knew your mother. Good woman."

My mother died after giving birth to Omar. I was four years old. When we were young, papa spoke about mama often and his eyes lit up when he talked about her, my mother Aurora, the only woman he ever loved. I wish she was not dead, was all I could think of in those years when papa got lonely and Omar became increasingly restless in his sleep so that I, at times, had to wake up in the middle of the night to cradle him in my arms and let papa have his rest so he could function at work the next day. I needed a mother too; I wanted to be taken care of by her. And it used to anger me, the way we were denied having a mother. But we coped, Omar and I. We survived, or I would like to think we did. But perhaps I am wrong. Maybe I was the one doing the surviving for him.

8

THE LAST TIME I WAS in San Jacinto was to attend papa's burial,
a year and nine months ago. I was not summoned when he
was dying, as though death was so ordinary that I should not
be bothered and should just carry on with my daily affairs. I
knew that old age had made him weak and prone to colds and
bronchitis but his refusal to see a doctor for a regular check-up
prevented us, or me, rather—for I am always the last to know
of all the crucial things—from knowing his real state of health.
To be fair, he died in his sleep and it was not easy to get hold
of me in Los Angeles. There was no land line or cell phone
that they could immediately use, and Omar thought to take
care of the arrangements first. I would have loved to hear that
my father asked for me, or that he had some last words for
me, an important message, perhaps, that he failed to tell me
when he was still alive. But I was told nothing of that sort, so I
arrived home with a surge of guilt and regret because I found
him already lifeless inside a coffin. There was his final absence
about which nothing could be done, and I stood there like a
broken child, seeking his father's voice in a vast raucous world.
I should have spent more time with him, I thought. I should
not have chided him for his drinking but instead let him live
the remainder of his life the way he wanted. Immediately I
went over our earlier days, father and son, the early morning

rise and evening walks, the story-telling. I recalled his dirty finger nails and the way he went straight to the basin to wash his hands when he came home from the farm. I recalled too, a walk we took together one morning checking the Gmelina trees. In a year's time, he said, they would be ready for cutting. It was an ordinary tropical summer day. After about a forty-five-minute walk, we rested and found shade under the acacia trees. We drank the fresh coconut juice that we took with us. He told me how, as a young boy, there were days when he rose early to watch the river at dawn. There was a varying luster on the waters depending on where he stood, from behind a tree or over by the riverbank, while the sun slowly rose high above the clouds. Across the river, down by the bottomlands, was a large area of wildflowers and further down, if you walked past the towering weeds and ragged shrubbery, you would come to a clearing. He went there simply to witness all these, nothing more. But the river had dried many years ago before I was born, and papa talked about the loss of the river as if the loss was his own. "At times it is hard to believe, that we are, at present, in the future that we once spoke of in the distant past. The future that I speak of, is where we are now, when some of our thoughts begin with the words when we were young. For you and I can sit on the wild grass and go over those tender years, retell versions of ourselves, when you and I, in varying times, were children once," he said. I remembered how his face looked calm, like all traces of a hard life were tempered by the sun's streaks filtering through the trees. As though resting his back against the trunk was all that a man needed to break free from whatever it is that chained him.

Standing in front of papa's coffin, I remembered all these moments, oblivious of the crowd that gathered at his wake. I touched his face and did not want to let go. Maybe it was my guilt, maybe it was the way I tried to recall what our last words were to each other, but I couldn't be certain what they were. What was it I felt, standing there, facing death in the eye? It was hollowness, and I wanted to bask in its vacant chambers. I plagued myself with questions. Did I squander too much time? Did I thank my father enough? What words could have been exchanged between us, what was it that we failed to tell each other?

Meanwhile, the crowd at his wake got bigger. Like most wakes in the barrio, people played cards and gambled. They ate and drank liquor and spoke loudly. The usual words of condolences were spoken.

"I am sorry for your loss."

"He is in a better place."

"He had a really good heart."

But none of these words were comforting. I nodded my head in response to their sympathy. But I was the one in grief and who needed indulging. I wanted neither sympathy nor pity. What I wanted was to be left alone. On the last evening of his wake, I stepped away from the crowd and headed towards the road, faltering in the dark as though I arrived at a place where I didn't know anyone. Not even myself.

9

I KNOW MOST OF papa's mornings began with a heartache even in those fulgent days when the sun drowned the land with perfect light. It was there, the sorrow, deep and present. It was there as the sea diffused its salty air before the smog and dust began to invade. It was there when he rose from his bed and opened the back door to check, first, if the garden needed watering, and second, if the bamboos had finally flowered. It was there when he paused to look at us still asleep on the floor before he left for work. Heaven only knows the laments of his heart. It was there still, that sorrow, ingrained like an invisible gene born with the body. Most of his mornings, if not all of them, were that way, for such was the lot of those fathers, the ones who ached in silence for what they couldn't provide their children.

A specter of my father appears to me unprompted, or perhaps I will myself to see him. And here is papa waking up at five in the morning, fumbling at the back of the hut, cradling his rooster. He comes back inside, drinks cocoa, hums a tune. He steps out again, is gone momentarily, comes back and changes his clothes. He leaves for the hacienda and arrives home at around six in the evening. He rests and lies down on a bed of bamboo slats for about half an hour. He is tired, his back hurts.

Then he gets up, goes to the kitchen and prepares food. He leads the prayer before dinner and recounts the events of his day. There is nothing much new to tell about his day, for each day was the same as the rest of the other days. He is a farm worker, a *sacada*. He is out in the fields all day wearing a thin long sleeve cotton shirt to protect him from cuts and a shirt wrapped around his head to protect him from the sun. With a machete, he plants or weeds the cane or slashes away the stalks that stand as tall as 20 feet. He cleans the stalks and lines them up in rows in the fields. Then he carries them on his shoulders and takes them to the trucks. Or he pours the fertilizers on the soil with his bare hands. There is something to be admired about a man who takes pride in his work no matter how menial it seems, who empties his whole heart into his labor like it is something sacred, as though the act of bending to pick up the stalks and putting them on his shoulders is itself an act of prayer. He thrives in this kind of industriousness, this devotion to work no matter how his body suffers from the strenuous exertions. He believed that what makes a man is showing up to work each day with devotion.

Here is also papa riding a *bangka,* a long narrow boat. Between the months of June to September, the dead season when work in the hacienda is scarce, he goes fishing so we have something to eat. Somehow papa always managed to come home with something for us. Sometimes he gave up his portion so Omar and I could have more.

There are small treats, of course. Some nights the three of us all go outside, sit on the bamboo bench, and delight at the stars in the sky. Then he tells stories. He whistles. He jokes around. He sings his favorite ballad, *Matud Nila* (They Say):

Matud nila ako dili angay
Nga magmamanggad sa imong gugma,
Matud nila ikaw dili malipay,
Kay wa ako'y bahanding nga kanimo igasa,
Gugmang putli mao day pasalig
Maoy bahanding labaw sa bulawan

They say that I must not
Desire for your love
They say that you will not be happy
As I have no treasure to offer you
Pure love is all I promise
A treasure more precious than gold

He said he used to sing this to mama during their courtship. "That is how she fell for me," papa said. And Omar and I laughed because he couldn't carry a tune. Papa never remarried, he stayed faithful to our mother to the very end. And this I should say about my father, that he was a faithful man.

When I retrace his steps, ponder the past generations, the history is too familiar. His father also worked at the hacienda, a lifetime of labor that bore no future or fortune for him and his family. Father's older brother, Julio, died of pneumonia at the age of ten. There was no medical care available, or if there was any, they could not afford it. He stayed at home and grew weaker and thinner each day. It was papa who found Julio lifeless in his sleep one afternoon. For three hours, papa wept beside his dead brother until his parents arrived. When Julio was alive, he worked so my father could go to school. A sacrifice had to be made within a family, that one sibling had to work to help pay for another's schooling; that was an unspoken rule. Papa went to school on and off and reached third grade. After Julio died, papa worked in the hacienda and never went to school again.

Often times I catch myself humming papa's favorite ballads because it is a memory of him that I love to remember. I also love those rainy nights when Omar and I listened attentively to his animated stories in the cramped space of our humble hut. All these come back to me especially when I breathe the scent of moist earth on a rainy day. Somehow all these come together, song and rain and papa's voice, and I long for a small, enclosed space, so I rush to the bedroom and shut the door, because back then, there was no space to run around, no room to be distant; we gathered in one place for that was all we had, and it was reassuring to turn to any side and find my family was right next to me. I suppose there is a memory that matters, a singular memory that reminds you of a world that is safe and comforting.

10

SISA IS A WOMAN in the novel *Noli Me Tangere* who went crazy when her two sons, Basilio and Crispin, were driven out of the convent after they were accused of stealing sacred objects from the church. The younger of the two boys, Crispin, was never found again after being interrogated by the *sacristan mayor* about the incident.

There is a woman in San Jacinto whom everyone calls Sisa. No one knows her real name. She looks disheveled; her dry hair is long and unkempt. She begs for change, and when you hold out your hand, she looks at your palm and reads your fortune. There was wild talk that she was a *manananggal*, an evil, vampire-like witch, as she was seen only during the day, and at night she was nowhere to be found. Nobody knew where she lived or where she slept. They claimed that at night she roamed around and preyed on her victims. As a child, I was afraid of the *manananggal*; some people have sworn that they have seen one. It was common to find households with garlic or salt placed near their doors because these items were supposed to ward them off. I never believed that to be true of Sisa. Instead, I found her to be misunderstood by everyone and I took pity on her. "Hey boy," she called out to me once when I was walking through the vacant lot behind the church looking for marbles. "Come here, let me see your palm," she said.

"I don't have money," I replied.

"Silly child! Of course you don't have money. I just want to take a quick look. There is some aura in you, something special. There is something about your future that needs to be looked into. Come closer. I will do no harm to you. Are you afraid of an old woman like me?"

"No! I am not afraid of you. I am not afraid of anyone."

Out of curiosity, I approached her and held out my right hand. She looked at my palm intently, studied it as though there was something there that caught her eye. She closed her eyes for about twelve seconds then looked at the sky while muttering words under her breath. Then she slowly let go of my hand.

"What is it? What do you see?" I asked.

"Oh, dear child, there is hope for you. You are going places. You will not stay in this forsaken town. But I see that your journey is of an unusual kind. I see darkness, too, some tragedy. Watch out, boy. Watch out for those closest to you. Believe me, boy. There's evil lurking everywhere. You gotta keep your eyes open, boy. Keep them open, you hear? One day you will come back to me and tell me that I was right. And I am always right, but nobody listens to me, you see."

"I am going to leave San Jacinto? Really? When? And where am I going?"

"Far away. Oceans and oceans away."

"But wait! What tragedy do you speak of? And what evil? Please, tell me more. I want to know more."

She laughed and began to walk away while mumbling unintelligible words.

"Please don't go away. I swear, I'm not like the others. I never doubted you. Where do you live? Can my brother and I come see you?"

"I have no home, boy. I will come find you."

She said nothing more and continued to go on her way. I told no one of my encounter with her. I left the vacant lot confounded by what she had said. Nobody knows where she is originally from. They say that she arrived in town one morning carrying plastic bags full of clothes and trinkets. She got off at the bus stop in the middle of the town square. Everyone noticed her as they did all outsiders. She walked unmindful of the stares and went straight to a *carenderia* and ate as though she had not tasted food for days. She spoke to one and no one spoke to her. One day she went on a rant, speaking to herself out loud. The story goes that her husband was imprisoned for a crime he was innocent of. Due to lack of money to get competent legal representation, the case was grossly mishandled. He died in prison. She lost her mind. Since then, she wandered from place to place asking if anyone had seen her husband, Claudio. She has been heard saying "Repent! Repent! Repent for your sins! The time is coming!" Oh Sisa, you wise, enlightened one!

I never made fun of her like most people did. They laughed at her and called her names. *Buang! Sisa buang!* There is so much baseness in our hearts. I would like to touch the back of her arm and ask her her real name. I would like to sit beside her, listen to her, peek inside her head, and catch whatever it is that incites sorrow. If she sat here with me now, what stories would she tell me? She ought to be the one laughing, she ought to be the one bestowed with grace. I think she read my destiny correctly when I was a boy. I want her to read my palm once more and tell me what is left of my harrowed life.

I asked Rico about her when we went about town. She is still alive, he said, very old now, and last he heard, she had taken refuge at some church somewhere. They let her stay there as long as she didn't cause trouble. No more of that fortune-telling nonsense, she was admonished. There was also talk about her practicing black magic, and that people came to her when they wanted someone harmed. The majority of the townsfolk shunned her all the more. But the church couldn't completely turn her away of course as it wouldn't be a Catholic thing to do.

I think of her now. I think of papa. I think of Omar. Come back, all of you. Come to me in my dreams, at least.

TIO ANDRES SHOULD BE HERE soon to give me the news about Don Rafael. He is not my uncle by blood, but he and papa have been best friends for so many years, they were like brothers, and Omar and I always looked up to him as an uncle. His wife, *Tia* Gloria, is the closest I had to a mother. Their three children—Jose, Arturo, Claudia—were our playmates. If we weren't told to fetch water from the well or do other chores, we spent the day outdoors. We played hide-and-seek. Sometimes we climbed mango trees and picked fruits or begged the *sacadas* to give us sugar cane. Jose and I, the oldest ones in the group, climbed coconut trees and drank *buko* juice. We picked *caimitos, manzanitas,* and *siniguelas.* We played *Bahay-Bahayan,* a role-playing game in which all of us would act out ordinary situations, like having dinner together and such. We used the fruits that we picked as the food to be served. We used leaves as plates and chewed the cane. At times we pretended that we were in school. Claudia was always the teacher. "Okay class, it's time for drawing. Draw anything you like." She always had pencils and paper that she managed to set aside with care. She got those from the nuns in the church who handed out supplies once every three months. Twice a year, a group of people from a non-profit organization came to town and gathered kids from all the barrios. They read parables from the bible. They taught us to write the letters of the alphabet and handed out picture books and school supplies which we were allowed to take home.

"Omar, stand up here in front and tell us about your drawing."

Omar drew fish swimming in the sea. He also drew the shore and the two of us making sand castles. Omar's drawings of the sea surprised me because he didn't swim. What was it about the water that appealed to him?

"This was one afternoon when the tide was low, and Benjamin and I caught fish and we placed them inside a jar filled with salt water. Then we made sand castles and later we released the fish back into the sea."

Something flares inside me, rekindling those years that were kind to us when we were children free of ill will and discord. Why is it that when we are young, we cannot wait to get older and let our life begin, as though adulthood is some sort of alchemy that we are so eager to get our hands on? And when we are older, adulthood besets us with nostalgia, and we pine for those long gone years.

11

THE NAMELESS CITY I conjured up in my head as a child became Los Angeles where I have resided for seven years now. My license in occupational therapy landed me an employer, a skilled nursing facility that sponsored me to come to the city. I arrived shivering in the autumn chill of November. Mrs. Cruz, the owner, arranged for me to be picked up at the airport by a woman named Anita. She had dyed her hair light brown, a Filipina I instantly presumed and which was later confirmed. It was awkward for me to be in a car with a stranger, and I had little propensity for small talk. She immediately bombarded me with questions; where was I from, how long had I worked as a therapist, was I single, etc. She missed speaking and cursing in our dialect so she was happy that she was able to do that with me. She went on to tell me a brief history of her life before America. It is a story that is now familiar to me and often common to most immigrants from third world countries, one that begins with poverty. Slowly I became at ease with her as though we had met before or perhaps it was a sense of belonging to the same class that made me feel comfortable.

I was to stay for a while in a room in a house shared with other employees of the facility until further arrangements were made or until I could afford to find my own place. Anita treated me to a late lunch as by the time I got my luggage it was almost two in the afternoon, and I was indeed hungry. She insisted on taking me to Hollywood Boulevard, and I immediately thought that perhaps I'd see Sylvester Stallone or Tom Cruise in person. "Once you start working you won't have time to gallivant around. You have a week and a half before you start working so you should make use of those days sight-seeing," she said. Maybe it didn't cross her mind that I did not have the money to go places, but I didn't say anything. After our meal of burgers and fries, we walked along the boulevard teeming with all sorts of people who all looked beautiful to me. I was like a child, impressionable and wide-eyed at the big billboards and tall buildings. Anita took photos of me from almost every corner of the street and in front of the shops and fancy cars. I posed like one of those excited tourists keen on documenting their travels through photographs. There was a moment or two, amidst the bustle of the new world I had just stepped into, that I came close to tears as I was happy and in disbelief at the turn of my fate, that I, the once impoverished boy from a small town that none of those walking the streets besides Anita had heard of, had come to live my dream. I didn't share with Anita my disappointment at not seeing any celebrity. It was during the drive from Hollywood to the house that I thought of papa and Omar. It occurred to me how far away I was from them now. I didn't care to look out the window and pay attention to the surroundings as I felt exhausted, cold, and wanted to close my eyes. Anita asked me if I was all right, if there was anything I needed to buy, toiletries and such, so we could stop by a store. I shook my head for my exhaustion left me no desire to think about the things I needed and the thought of going to a store did not appeal. I fell asleep for most of the drive. Anita woke me up when we arrived at the two-storey house on Linden street. No one was home at that time. She led me to my room upstairs then showed me the rest of the house but didn't stay long and told me she would be back for me in the morning and take me out for breakfast. After she left, I took out the postcard I'd bought from one of the shops in Hollywood. I wrote a short note to papa and Omar: Arrived safely. Wish you were all here. Hope we will be together again soon.

Everything went well with my employment. On my first day of work, I met the owner, Mrs. Elena Cruz, whose hairdo reminded me of Imelda Marcos. Mrs. Cruz hailed from the island of Surigao del Norte and spoke Surigaonon, a language I do not speak or understand. After the difference in our native language was established, we spoke in English. She personally gave me a tour of the 154-bed facility. I had never been to a skilled nursing facility before so when I heard some screaming as we were walking down the hallway, it bothered me so much that I kept looking around to see where it had come from. Mrs. Cruz explained that those two patients screaming had dementia and were long-term residents. You will get used to it, she said. I had a week's training before I officially worked as an occupational therapist. Something about helping a patient regain their functioning abilities makes me proud of the work that I do. That I helped them develop skills for self-care such as feeding, dressing, and exercising, or that I recommended and taught them to use adaptive equipment to maximize their independence gave me a sense of purpose in the world. I deemed it was my life's meaning to help the elderly in that manner. Never mind that I sometimes got screamed at, or that they did not want me because of my thick accent or that I was a foreigner, and a host of other reasons that still leave me surprised or even shocked. These incidents did not escalate, however, as the patients were given the therapist they wanted, and I was assigned to other patients. Over time I have gotten used to these unpleasant episodes that I have learned to accept and have focused instead on other residents whose hearts I have won or those I became fond of.

One such patient that comes to mind is Jack Howard Skelly. Jack was admitted to the facility after having right hip replacement surgery. Every morning he looked forward to therapy. Employees and patients knew his boisterous laughter. He was a pleasant, well-travelled man who gave you random facts or data about anything while he was doing his exercises. "There are seven Japanese gods of good luck. Atilla the Hun died of nosebleed. A cat has four rows of whiskers. Women's hearts beat faster than men's. An olive tree can live up to 1500 years. Pearls melt in vinegar. Your hearing becomes less sharp after eating too much. Your thumb is the same length as your nose. A shrimp's heart is in its head." To test my Catholic knowledge, he asked me to enumerate the seven deadly sins. He found it amusing that I could only name five. He was admitted to our facility three days before Thanksgiving. No one visited him. "It's just me and Lola." Lola was his fat cat. He was our patient for two and a half months then he was discharged home. Almost two weeks later, he called me at work and asked me to pay him a visit at his house. He lived five miles away from the facility. I went to see him the following weekend. One visit turned into many and became a regular event. I would bring food or we'd have it delivered to his house. We watched old western movies. He introduced me to Cary Grant and Humphrey Bogart. If we weren't watching a film, we listened to Jobim or Sinatra or Nat King Cole and sometimes to opera, a type of music that I never managed to get into. He'd tell me about a recent book he'd read and let me have any book from his vast collection.

Strange how we may know important facts about someone and yet still know nothing about the person. The facts were such that Jack was seventy-one when he was admitted to the facility, that he lived in a three-bedroom bungalow located at 704 Warner Street, Los Angeles, that he had Aetna insurance and wished to be cremated. An advance directive was in place, a conservator was to be notified. And yet. There were nights when Jack and I would sit by the porch and it seemed as though I was sitting next to someone I hardly knew. For it was during those nights that I found myself listening to a man telling his life story, a man who, as a child, lived from one foster home to another, how one day when he was twenty-two, he received a call from someone named Wilbur claiming that Jack was his biological son, and all that Jack had said to Wilbur was "fuck you, get lost," then Jack hung up the phone. He never heard from Wilbur again and he didn't have any interest in knowing who his biological father was. I was listening to a man who once loved a woman until cancer took her away at the age of forty-nine, how he had never loved another woman since. He still kept all her belongings in the closet upstairs, even the two twenty-dollar bills she had left in her purse. Her name was Virginia. She had a miscarriage that made her ill and depressed so they both decided not to have any more children. It was a boy and they would have named him Clive Augustus. When there were moments that I caught Jack teary-eyed from nostalgia or some other longing, I'd tell him that he needed to rest now, that it was late and I had to get home. The truth was, I could not bear to see him in tears as I didn't know what to do or what to say to comfort him. I would drive home calling out to the gods to watch over Jack in his sleep, to ask that should anything happen to him he would not feel any pain. At the same time feelings of sadness and fear took over me, fear that I would grow old alone and lonely, that I would die not even knowing what it meant to be alive. Then I'd call Cora for no reason, just to know that she was there. "Are you okay," she'd ask. Perhaps my tone of voice gave me away, perhaps the oddness of my phone calls during those hours when I knew that she was busy writing notes on patients' charts made her suspect something. "Did you visit Jack tonight? Are you well? Do you want me to stop by before I head home?" I'd say yes, and her presence instantly gave me comfort.

Jack got pneumonia one winter and was admitted to the acute hospital. He then became prone to illness and infections and eventually got weaker. For some time I volunteered to do groceries for him, made him soups and sandwiches, took him out for short walks around his street. His memory was declining. He forgot names, the time and day of his favorite television shows, if he had taken his medicines, if the gardener came or not, if he paid the water bill, and so on. His then convivial disposition changed into a pensive one so that at times I could not tell if his mind was empty or if he was in an otherworldly state. He was no longer keen on telling the motley tales of his world travels. Instead, lethargy took over so that he often retired to bed earlier than usual. I insisted on arranging for a full-time caregiver for him and was glad that he obliged without hesitation.

The very last time I heard Jack's boisterous laugh was during his birthday on a cold January day. Two of the nurses and another therapist who took care of him when he was our patient went with me to his house at lunchtime. We brought him a birthday cake and gave him a big card signed by all the staff. He was teary-eyed reading through all the birthday notes. I spent half of the afternoon with him. I relished our earnest exchanges and was happy to have seen him in a jovial mood as that afternoon was to be the last of those exchanges. He passed away on a rainy evening in February, three weeks after his birthday. He passed away in his sleep. That was how he wanted to die, quietly, in his own bed, in the house where he had lived for forty-three years.

12

I LIVE IN A ONE-BEDROOM apartment on Keystone Street. I live on the second floor and have a balcony that faces the narrow alley where I see houses, the back of apartment buildings, and occasional bums digging through the dumpsters. Every now and then when I am on the balcony, a bum would yell and ask for change. I would shake my head because the only change I kept around the apartment was enough for my laundry on weekends, and, also, I found most of them to be able-bodied and strong enough to manage long stretches of walk, and I wondered why they do not get a job while I, the immigrant, work hard to earn my keep. Where are their families? I used to ask myself during my one and a half years of living in Los Angeles, but after a while, I got so used to seeing them that I stopped wondering. On weekends when I am not working, I stay at home, take long naps, and watch action movies. I take two strolls a day. One after breakfast and another in the late afternoon or after dinner depending on the weather. In one of those evening strolls, I had a craving for a cold beverage, so I went to a donut shop a block away from my apartment. That was when I first met Sang, the friendly Cambodian owner. It was about five minutes before closing so I rushed to get in. He smiled and told me to take my time, and I said I was just going to buy some cold beverage and that it wouldn't take long. "No, it's okay," he insisted, and said that I should not worry because after he closed the store, it would only take him fifteen minutes to get home since there was no more traffic. "Besides," he added, "my family is away for a night to visit relatives in San Bernardino, so I am in no hurry to go home to a quiet house." He was reading a book when I got in and I asked him what book that was just to have some small talk as a gesture of appreciation for his pleasantries. It was about Buddhism.

"Do you like to read? Do you write? Are you a writer?" he asked.

"Yes, I enjoy reading books and no, I am not a writer. Why do you ask?"

"Well, you never know who you encounter in this town. I ask because I want someone to write my story."

"Your story? Personal story? Fiction?"

We ended up chatting for hours under the dim light of his closed shop called Dara's Donuts named after his first child. His story began on a Saturday morning in Cambodia, the usual family gathering at his grandfather's house. It was a tradition, five families bringing food and treats, eating together, laughing, teasing, doing regular things that families do. Then there was a loud banging on the door, a voice yelled that they were going to break down the door if they did not open it. His grandfather opened the door and was met by men pointing guns at him. Sang said they were the Khmer Rouge. I did not know about the Khmer Rouge then but from the way Sang described them, I had the impression that they were rebels or a kind of a vigilante group. I pretended to have heard about the group and let him carry on with his story. "Life was never the same since that day," he said, and what was so strong in his mind all throughout his harrowing experience was that his grandfather told him to escape to Thailand, and he made Sang promise that that's what he would do. Sang did not know the way to Thailand. The only thing he knew was that he just had to keep heading west and he would arrive there at some point. It was that promise paired with the will to survive that gave him the strength to battle his silent companion, despair. He was eighteen then, hardly a man, separated from the rest of his family. During his escape, he passed through farmlands, forests, and mountains and slept on the soil and a bed of leaves. He ate wild bananas and papayas and whatever food he was able to steal when he sneaked into people's empty houses. Dead bodies became a common sight. At times he travelled with fellow escapees who later got sick or gave up altogether. When he told me the story, he often looked blankly through the glass, the passing cars on Arden Street visible from where he sat. I felt that he looked past the normal stirrings outside, past the pedestrians walking under a bright moon but instead, he looked straight into the window of the darkest period of his life.

After all the numerous imprisonments and escapes, he finally arrived in Thailand, and from there came to America. Sang went to the kitchen and made tea for both of us. Our talks transitioned to other things, and it was as if we were two old friends who had not kept in touch for many years and were now catching up for lost time. We were so immersed in our conversation that we had not noticed how late it was. An immediate bond was formed between us that evening.

When I got home, I looked up Khmer Rouge on the internet and felt feelings of tenderness for Sang. I made an effort to see him every weekend, for not only did I enjoy his company, but I also admired his character, his resilience, and cheerful disposition. Over time I met his wife and three children. I got invited to birthdays and holidays, especially Thanksgiving and Christmas. Sang was the first true friend I had in Los Angeles. Our age difference was not an impediment. He said that I reminded him of himself when he was my age, when he was a young man who knew no one and nothing about America. "No one understands an immigrant better than a fellow immigrant," he said. At once we were brothers at heart.

Once in a while he came to my apartment to have a smoke or drink one bottle of Corona beer before he drove home. Three years later, he and his family moved to Pomona where they bought a house. He closed the shop and opened a new one closer to their new home. We seldom saw each other after they moved. The donut shop was unoccupied for four months after it was closed, and whenever I passed by it on my evening walks, I thought of Sang, our conversations, his lovely family. Sometimes when the security guard manning the property was not in sight, I peeked through the glass to see if the bench that we often sat on was still there, then I'd spread my palms on the glass as if touching it immediately brought me back to those pleasant evenings. I often felt nostalgic walking back home, and when I got inside my apartment, I headed straight to the balcony, sat on the folding chair even when the evenings were cold, and waited for the hours to pass or for loneliness to wane.

Many nights were like that since Sang and his family moved, and it was then that I began to feel what isolation was like in a city that was always alive with something, alive with music and words, drenched with hope and industry and expression. I searched for myself in the city of my dreams but what I found were questions, empty spaces, the dim light of bare houses. Is this what I came here for? I waited for answers to come to me in a form that I could recognize but there was nothing, only emptiness, the vast sky, the deep night that seemed to have grown tired of my meanderings. I often retired to bed feeling cold and somewhat sad, and I left the curtains undrawn for the way the moonlight seeped through my bedroom window gave me comfort.

Since I started living on my own, I have gotten into the habit of writing my thoughts. This first came about when I had idle time during my bus rides and continued long after I bought my first car, an old Toyota Corolla, from a co-worker. I filled notebooks with random musings when I was at coffee shops, on my balcony, on benches while waiting for my clothes to dry. Re-reading the contents of the notebook, I found that I did not write in regular intervals. I wrote when I was at the height of emotions or when something struck me quite intensely. For instance, one sunlit afternoon, I sat on the steps leading to my apartment. While I looked out into the street full of parked cars, a feather floated in midair directly above me. I gazed at the feather's descent, slow but graceful. Staring at its gradual fall, in my mind I was certain that it was going to land on my left foot. But that did not happen, for it finally rested on the step below my feet, and strange then that from that occurrence, I wrote how I was often inaccurate, how often I was let down by my own heightened anticipations. On another day, I wrote about the bare branches of trees in January, how striking the way the shards of light slid through the narrow spaces in between branches, how I wondered if trees ache being living things, and if they did, what did they weep about? I wonder if I am alone in these absurd curiosities? I wrote about the dead leaves caught in the cobwebs on the iron railings of my window, or the sight of a hummingbird hovering above the primrose. Perhaps these thoughts were the product of a lonely life, when one is devoid of deep personal connections and thus bound to pay attention to the little details that often go unnoticed. I wrote about random encounters with people.

Once, heeding the call of the sea, I went to Venice beach. I sat on a patch of grass facing the water where behind me, the cacophony of music and mindless prattle ensued at the boardwalk. An old man wearing tattered clothes sat a foot away from me. From his appearance and smell, I assumed he was homeless. We both looked out into the sea, and I wondered what was on his mind, which roads his dirty feet had treaded on in recent days, for I did have a strange curiosity about the life of the vagabond. He then lay on his back with his arms under his head and said, "What a beautiful day! This is all I need." I feared that he would go on a ramble and I was relieved that that was all he said and did not engage in a conversation for I was not in the mood to chat. What moved me was hearing the man appreciate beauty. That was the reality he chose to see in that moment, not the gash on his right foot nor the question of where home would be that night. Our mute encounter consoled me. I felt inexplicably light as the nameless stranger who remained unaware of his words' impact on me continued to gaze at the sky. Random thoughts of these sorts were often in my notebooks. Whenever I read them I got reacquainted with myself, as though the self who wrote those words in that particular time in the past was no longer the same person reading them in the present.

Every year around Thanksgiving, I drive up north to San Simeon and stay there for a couple of days. Something about the place draws me there. Perhaps it is the unhurried pace. I suppose the gaiety close to Christmas makes me feel lonely and drives me to sulk in the quietude of San Simeon. I was there when Omar ventured into the sea never to return. That autumn morning of my second day there, I took photos of the sky, the sea, the lone seagull in the offing. I stood by the pier musing over dissonance between myself and others; broken by human frailties thrown at me, or by me, unknowingly. What prompted me to be in that mood was remembering the confrontation that Omar and I had at papa's wake. I recalled the look he gave me, a fuming glance as though something I did revolted him.

"Did it save us, Benjamin?" His voice seethed with anger.

"What? Listen, Omar, forgive me if I—"

"No, do not bother explaining," he said curtly.

"I am sad too. I am also suffering like you," I said.

"And what do you know about suffering, Benjamin? You were never around. You and your grandiosity, your delusions."

"Do not be quick to judge me. You do not know what I went through or go through every day while you are thinking that I am just having the time of my life there, living grandiosely as you put it."

"Really? How convenient for you to say that when the rest of us here actually suffered while you were in the States living out your dream world. You thought of no one but yourself. No one. You have been blind, Benjamin, and you still are. Blind to what is really happening around you."

"I see. So nothing counts, Omar? Not the food on the table, the medicines, the house, the money I sent for your schooling that you spent on booze and god knows what else."

He said that nobody asked me to do that, that he and papa managed even without my contribution, that none of it mattered in the end because it did not save us. Before I could ask what he meant by nothing saved us, he hurled all sorts of names at me—the selfish, ruthless, treacherous drifter that I was—and I felt slighted at his accusations. Drifter, I concede, but treacherous? I demanded to know what he meant by treacherous, and in that acrimonious exchange of ours, we turned into the strangers that we had become to each other. What had we really learned about each other over the years with the few letters we exchanged and my short visits? In the last letter I received from him, he inquired when I was coming home, that papa, as of late, had been ill. I replied and told him to immediately take papa to the doctor and that I could not yet give him a definite date of when I could come home for a visit. That was the last time I heard from him until papa passed away.

How dare you, I yelled at him inside my head, *how fucking dare you dismiss my suffering.*

"And what about you, Omar? What contributions or heroic deeds have you done to save us, whatever the hell you mean by that? Since you are so keen to put me down and I get no ounce of respect from you, why don't you tell me what you have made of your life? Do you wake up at 5:30 in the morning to get ready for work, work that you have to do not just to support yourself but also your family because if you don't do it, god knows what's going to happen to them, god knows there is no one else who would step up and take responsibility? Heck, I've worked two jobs when I had to, and not once did I lecture you about how to live your life, not once did you hear me say anything about how you're living it in utter waste and here you are grossly accusing me of ridiculous things."

A jab—that was the response I got from Omar. It landed on my right jaw. I was too stunned to move or fight back, but I didn't have a chance to respond to him in whatever way for he immediately stormed out of the house. He didn't come home for three nights. By then my keenness to have a conversation with him had abated. But I knew he had been home when I was out of the house, or asleep, for I saw bottles of beer left on the table or next to the bin, clearly a message that he was avoiding me. He knew my departure date but that didn't urge him to show up, say goodbye or even leave a note. I left San Jacinto two days earlier than planned and stayed in Sugbu. I couldn't wait to get back to Los Angeles, bury myself with work, eager to forget the life I left behind in San Jacinto.

After a day of wandering about taking photographs, I went to a bar called Staten. It was a short distance to the motel where I stayed. I sat in between a skinny guy wearing a funky hat, and a middle-aged looking woman clad in a red flimsy top. The man turned to me and nodded his head. I lifted my glass as if motioning a toast to something, though there was nothing to toast, nothing at all that I could have conjured out of my own restless mind.

"What's up, man? You from around here?" the man asked.

"No. I live in L.A. Just here for a few days."

"For work or pleasure?"

"Just needed to get away from the city for a few days."

"Yeah, I hear you, dude. L.A. can be harsh. It can be a bitch. Lived there for a while. Lived with a girlfriend for two and a half years until she ran off with this rich old dude, and I mean really old? Fat, ugly, clearly had those hair implants, you know? Drove a Porsche or one of those fancy sports cars that looked tiny for him because this bloke was super huge. Obviously looking for a trophy girlfriend. Broke me when she left, man. Hard not to be jaded after that. Cause you know, like, I thought we were in this really amazing, no bullshit relationship? We had this deep connection. You ever felt that way with someone, like in a deep soul level? Like it's karmic and shit? Know what I mean? Like it's awesome, right? Anyway, we always managed not having enough money. Like always on the verge of poverty but never came to a point where we got homeless or had nothing to eat? But I guess she got fed up with that kind of life. You know, she wanted to have things that people around her had. You know like a keeping up with the Joneses syndrome or something like that, whatever. All this materialistic crap. But I kinda understood, really. I mean, she had her dreams too, you know. We all do. But I wasn't like the man who could make it happen for her. I'm just a simple dude. You know what I mean? Like I'm happy if I play my guitar and find other people to jam with. And next thing you know you're just playing with people you don't even know, and you get into this rhythm then you smoke a bit of weed and start talking and laughing. It's the coolest thing ever. And she just changed too like I think L.A. changes you in a way, kinda fucks you up if you allow yourself to get carried away with the bullshit and all? Know what I mean? She used to be this sweet down-to-earth girl and that all disappeared. Anyway, so yeah, L.A., man."

"Yes, yes. Life in L.A. can be tough."

I did not want to further the conversation. I did not want to speak at all. Perhaps I relayed that message in my facial expression or obvious lack of enthusiasm for he said nothing more after that. I looked around and scanned the faces in the room. It seemed that what I saw there was what I saw anywhere in Los Angeles—people with eyes that comb for connection. Before me was a throng of things lost—dreams, selves, innocence, the love of your life. And there too was the manifestation of things found—escape, amusement, diversion, a new friend or lover perhaps. The customers seemed to enjoy the house music. The lady in red stood up and danced all by herself. I left the bar after having three glasses of beer and went back to the motel. I opened the balcony's sliding door wishing for a waft of salty breeze. I turned on the small radio on the bedside table. Starry, Starry Night was the song that played, and I sang along and sipped the bottle of wine that I brought with me for the trip. How lonely the world seemed as I sat on the comfy queen size bed, wide-eyed in the dark. I attempted to clear my mind but the more I willed myself to let go of all thoughts, some vague memory kept turning up. One of the memories was of an old acacia tree, the one that Omar and I passed when we walked from home to the town square and vice-versa. The story passed down to us about that acacia tree was that it was haunted, that a *kapre* lived there with a habit of snatching misbehaving kids. Whenever we were three feet away from that tree in the dark of night, Omar and I started running as fast as we could for fear that the *kapre* might snatch either one of us. We promised not to abandon each other, that should one be snatched, then the one left behind should plead with the *kapre* that he would have to come along. Then we thought of papa and how sad he would be if he lost both of us. We resolved to always be good kids so the *kapre* would leave us alone.

That evening was somber. Autumn had cast a fit of gloom. I stepped out of the room and went to the balcony. A brown butterfly emerged out of nowhere, flitting along and finally landing on the railings. In my culture, the superstition goes that a brown butterfly denotes the spirit of a dead loved one. Could it have been Omar embodied in the brown butterfly? It stayed still as though it found a resting place. There we were on a chilly November evening, the butterfly and I, in a fleeting moment of odd confrontation, in what seemed like a silent exchange of a secret language. I moved closer to the butterfly and wanted to touch it with my hand. Alas, it flew away into the night.

Due to bad reception or that my mobile phone was tuned off, no one was able to get hold of me all those days when I was in San Simeon as my brother's dead body lay on the shore. While I was delighted to wake up to the sound of seagulls and ate eggs benedict for breakfast at a quaint café, *Tio* Andres and *Tia* Gloria identified my brother's body as that of their nephew, Omar Jose Aragon, son of now deceased Pablo and Aurora Aragon, brother of Benjamin Aragon who resides in America. "Yes, yes, that is Omar without a doubt. That cross pendant is his, was his mother's actually, but he never took that necklace off." "Oh, I have known him since he was a baby. He was a fine boy". While I sought comfort in San Simeon's quietude, *Tio* Andres and *Tia* Gloria scrambled to look for money to take care of the mortuary arrangements by reaching for the shoebox hidden under their bed where they kept whatever little money they saved. They did not deem it proper to rummage through our possessions and sell whatever could be sold—books, shelves, vases, plates, clothes—to be able to come up with some money. Aware that their own savings were not enough, they immediately went to the municipal hall to speak to the mayor and ask for help. "He has a brother in America who can repay the money you lend," they both assured Mayor Diaz. The mayor handed them six hundred eighty-five pesos, money he took from his desk's drawer, and told them to come back in four days. When they left the municipal hall, *Tia* Gloria went to the hut. Her instinct told her that there was something of importance that she would find there. And indeed there was, for on the table was a box with an envelope on top of it addressed to *Tio* Andres/*Tia* Gloria/Benjamin. It contained his instructions and a key to the box containing money that was more than enough to cover all expenses. In fact, they were shocked that Omar was able to save that much. How long had he been planning this? There was no note of apology or explanation, just a straightforward list of things to be done. He did not want a wake. He wanted to be cremated immediately. A contact person was listed and this person was to make all the necessary arrangements. He knew there wasn't going to be a Mass for him. *Tio* Andres and *Tia* Anita prayed over his body before it was taken away to be cremated. Townsfolk sighed and questioned and speculated.

"What was he doing swimming alone at night?"

"Was he alone or did he have company?"

"He never got over his papa's death."

"He is in heaven now with his parents."

"I just saw him last week playing his guitar."

"Did he not have a girlfriend from another town?"

"His poor brother, all alone now."

"Was he drunk? He smoked marijuana, you know."

"Why cremation?"

"There's more to this than we know."

"Now that I think about it, he was a little odd, a bit of a loner, aloof at times."

Tio Andres and *Tia* Gloria did not know where to get an urn for his ashes. They found nothing in the house that they could use so when they received Omar's ashes in a temporary urn, they left it that way for three days until *Tia* Anita chanced upon a decent jar at the flea market. All this took place while I sought refuge in San Simeon's autumn sky wallowing in sentimentality. All this was relayed to me over the phone while I stopped to eat at a diner on my drive back to Los Angeles. How they managed to get hold of me escaped my inquiry, for the moment I heard *Tio* Andres' sad voice, I knew I was about to hear distressing news. I thought that Omar was in some sort of trouble with the law, or that he got into an accident perhaps, but death, death did not even enter my mind.

"We have been trying to get hold of you for days. It's Omar. Something terrible has happened. His body has washed ashore. You need to come home right away."

"Washed ashore? What do you mean, *Tio*?"

"I mean, he's, he's dead, Benjamin. Your brother is dead."

14

THAT MORNING WHEN I ARRIVED at Don Rafael's house for the very first time, I was met by a servant, *Manang* Lita, a plump woman in her early fifties. Her face was greasy, and she wore a checkered apron over a flower-printed duster. I could tell she was in a rush by the rapid pace of her steps, her anxious look, and the way she did not bother with a casual chat. I expected the usual questions of where was I from, who my parents were, how many siblings did I have, etcetera. I was glad that she did not care to ask. She knew my name, which meant that she had been advised of my arrival. She asked if I had eaten breakfast as she led me inside the house. I said "yes," regrettably, after I smelled the aroma of garlic rice. She said that Don Rafael was entertaining guests from the city who arrived a day earlier than expected. She said one of the servants left two days ago after receiving news about an illness in the family. She was glad I arrived that day for she could use my help. I put my plastic bag containing my clothes on a wooden stool in the kitchen where she had resumed her tasks. She cooked pork and chicken *adobo* and another dish made of fish. She handed me a plate of *pansit* and a large *pandesal*. "There will be endless activity in the kitchen as long as the guests are still here so you better not have an empty stomach."

I ate quietly. I thought of Omar and wished that he had some of the food especially since he was not feeling well when I left. When I felt full, I stood up to get a glass of water. "Do you want orange juice? Milk? Have some milk. A boy your age needs milk. Go on, it's in the fridge." I don't remember drinking milk at home, but I obeyed her. She instructed me to tidy up the rooms on the second floor and to make sure the pillows had clean pillow cases.

"Do some dusting too. Grab the feather duster in the supply room. Bring a pail of water and cloth and use it to wipe anything that's made of glass. And be careful with those lamps and vases. They are very valuable. They cost way more than both our lives combined. Antiques, passed on for generations."

I nodded and went for the feather duster and took a pail out of the supply room.

"You didn't even finish your food. Are you sure you're full?"

"Yes, I am, *Manang* Lita. I ate *pandesal* before coming over here. I'll save the leftovers for later."

"You must eat, child. You're skin and bones. And you never have to worry about food in this house. Don Rafael is generous like that. He doesn't want us to starve. We eat what he eats, everything in the fridge is for everyone. I tell you, I was once *kusinera* at another *haciendero's* household, and our food was different from theirs. We had the cheapest dried fish and corn. Their leftovers were fed to the dogs, but sometimes, when the lady of the house had visitors, she'd tell us to finish their leftovers, but I suspect it was only to put up a front to her friends showing them that she was kind and good to us. And those were the only times, when guests were present, that we were able to eat their food. But in this household, you will get fat. I gained weight after just a few months of being here.

Anyway, never mind the pail of water, it might be heavy for you to carry. Just use the cloth and feather duster."

"Okay."

"Oh wait. I should send you to the market first before you start cleaning the rooms upstairs."

She sent me off to the market and gave me a small purse with money in it and a list of what to buy. She told me to ride with *Manong* Ramon, the driver, who was going to the town square to buy ice, beer, and liquor. She stepped out briefly to talk to *Manong* Ramon, and when she came back, we walked together to the garage where she pointed to a silver Mercedes Benz. *Manong* Ramon's head peeked out of the window and he motioned for me to get in the vehicle.

Our drive to the market was a quiet one. He asked me where I was from. He told me to wait for him by the shed right before the bus stop on the side of the market entrance. I said okay, and we spoke of nothing else. It was six days before the annual town fiesta. The town square was already full of fanfare; locals and out-of-towners filled the streets, floats were being prepared for the parade, groups of young men and women were practicing their Sinulog dance in the open. It was strange catching a glimpse of it all from the window of the car. When we reached the market, I got out of the car and went straight to the stalls to buy the items. I had no trouble finding all the vegetables that *Manang* Lita listed for I had been to the wet market before on other occasions and was familiar with it. I approached a stall that sold vegetables and gave the *tindera* the list and she put them all together under eight minutes. I did not loiter for fear that *Manong* Ramon would scold me if I was not already at the shed when he showed up. Our drive home was again devoid of conversation. It was only when we arrived at the mansion and I was about to disembark from the car that he finally said: "Well, son, I guess I'll be seeing you around." I nodded and got out of the car carrying the two plastic bags from the market. I handed the bags and purse to *Manang* Lita, and then went my way to start my chores upstairs.

I passed by the spacious living room and saw two long custom-made sofas. One seated about twelve people, and the other, six. There was an upright piano and two large bookshelves. There was a mini bar in the corner next to the stairs. The second floor also had a living room though smaller in size than the one downstairs. There were shelves filled with books and picture frames. The photos were of Don Rafael's lineage, all Spanish *mestizos* and *mestizas*. His grandfather on his father's side was once the town mayor of San Jacinto. A photo of his induction to the office was framed and hung on the wall. Large black and white photos filled the hallways. Each bedroom had a dresser and side table, the beds without sheets, the pillows without covers. I did my tasks without any incident. Once in a while I looked out the window and got a good view of Don Rafael's vast hacienda. I heard birds chirp now and then. There was also music, some form of dance, tango or waltz; I could not distinguish one from the other. After I finished with my chores upstairs, I joined *Manang* Lita in the kitchen. The rest of the afternoon was filled with more chores. By eight in the evening *Manang* Lita sent me off to bed and it was not until the following day that I met Don Rafael.

The servants' quarters were about four hundred meters behind the main house. Those who slept there at night were— *Manang* Lita, *Manang* Perla, and *Manang* Ines. *Manang* Lita was the cook. *Manang* Perla did the laundry. *Manang* Ines, the one who took the emergency leave, did the general household cleaning. *Manong* Ramon did not live far away so he went home every night but sometimes stayed over if Don Rafael requested him to do so. I slept in a small room in the ground floor of the main house, tasked to attend to Don Rafael in case he needed something at night.

Don Rafael's wife, Dona Isabelle, passed away from a car accident eight years before I came to live in their household. It was a case of a drunk driver falling asleep at the wheel and colliding with the car she was driving. She died instantly while the other driver lived. They did not have children. She once had a miscarriage, a boy, and did not get pregnant again. Everyone missed her and spoke highly of her. I was told that Don Rafael never stopped grieving over her death.

Of course I remember the very first time I met Don Rafael. I remember it distinctly as though no time had elapsed. I could not forget the way he shook my hand and how that gesture made me admire him for I did not think that a man of his stature had to shake a servant's hand. It was the same day when we first went on a stroll, when the promise of education was conveyed. All in a matter of a few hours, I had given him my absolute trust and respect.

In the first few weeks, I paid careful attention to Don Rafael's ways and routine. He was particular about certain things. On a typical day when he had no guests, he took his *siesta* at one-thirty in the afternoon. At around five, he wanted a clean ash tray, a glass, bottle of bourbon, and a deck of cards on the veranda where he played Solitaire for an hour. He would lounge there for another hour and a half, read a book and listen to music, or simply sit there in the quiet. He ate dinner at six-thirty. He had wine with his food. A clean ashtray should be brought to the dining table placed opposite his wine glass.

He was not finicky about food and did not complain about what was served. He drank more than he ate. He would go to his bedroom around eleven in the evening, and one would see him at seven-thirty the next morning drinking coffee on the veranda.

When I was finished with my evening chores and walked to my room to rest, sometimes I would catch Don Rafael standing by the veranda looking out into the expanse as if confronting the great darkness. I would pause and watch from behind the window sill, observing the ways of an important man, perhaps also trying to catch the little details of his life when no one was paying attention. I wondered, too, what occupied his thoughts, wondered if the quality of the quiet in San Rafael was what he preferred more than the haste of the big city. I have never had such fascination and curiosity about someone then that I would continue to watch him though he did nothing but stand or sit on his favorite chair with a drink, smoke his cigar, and occasionally whistle. I watched him until I got tired and then I would retreat to the silence of my own room.

It was in the afternoons on the veranda that he and I spent most of our time together. It was there that I knew what he was like as an only child, how he felt lonely, he said, having no kids his age to play with and converse. He attended elementary and high school at a private school in Manila. He had not made up his mind about what course to take in college so after graduating from high school at sixteen, he took a sabbatical for a year or so and came home to Sugbu. He said that all he wanted to do was paint, a hobby that his father, Don Luisito, met with displeasure for what he desired for him was to stop wasting time and proceed immediately to law school. "It is good to

have a lawyer in the family and it's beneficial to the business,"
his father said. Don Rafael had no desire of becoming a lawyer
and this caused a strain in their relationship. They quarreled
often, but an unexpected visit from his *abuelita* from Spain put
a sudden end to their spat. She intervened and Don Luisito
left him alone. Since then, he spent a lot of time in San Jacinto
where he did most of his paintings during those years. He said
that the sunrise beaming over the fields often inspired him,
and when the morning rays tapped his bedroom window, he
immediately rose and went straight to his canvas and painted
at the veranda.

To appease his father, he went with him when he made
rounds in their *haciendas*, learning the trade along the way
and developing a love for it. He took up business in college
thinking it was the more sensible choice as he was going to
inherit the family business. Before he went to the university, he
spent a year abroad, Spain, mostly, and some parts of Europe.
I listened to him in awe for a boy of my social rank had never
interacted with someone like him. And he was a great story-
teller, theatrical in his gestures. It was then that my lessons
began. He taught me how to write the alphabet. He made me
fill each page with one letter, big and small, beginning with
letter A and so on, and instructed me not to go beyond the
lines. During *siesta* when there was no work to be done in the
household, I practiced writing each letter in a notebook that
he gave me. And it was in those afternoons too that my love
affair with books began. He let me pick any book from the
shelf and let me read the first paragraph aloud. I had trouble
reading, of course, pronounced words slowly and incorrectly,
but he did not mind. He corrected any word I mispronounced
and told me what it meant. He let me read the pages aloud

until I got familiarized with the words and read them right. Since then, I looked forward to the times we spent reading or when he would tell me what the book was about and who the characters were. I listened intently, sitting on the cozy futon on the veranda that took in the afternoon light beautifully. During those times, I often sat in a daze imagining myself to be a character in a book, often the hero saving someone or solving a crisis. There were occasions where I would remain there on the veranda long after the sun had set, when all the lights outside were turned on, and from a distance, the house looked like a bright ship at night in the sea. And how far I let myself go then, for there were many months where I did not go home on weekends to see papa and Omar. By then I was in school, eager to study my lessons and do homework. I was too exhausted to travel home on Friday or Saturday and come back again to Don Rafael's house on Sunday. It seemed like there was always a reason not to go home: homework, household chores, rain, my faked illness. Perhaps I had changed, perhaps this was why Omar said to me on many occasions that I had become a different person but I was not consciously aware of it myself.

"How am I different?"

"You're no fun anymore. You don't play with us as much as you used to. Why are you keen to go back there? What's over there? The people you live with are all old."

"It's only temporary. Just for school. I'll always come back for you."

It was the last summer before I was to begin college in Sugbu that I spent the entire two months at home with Omar and papa. It became apparent to me that Omar had no interest in school and all he wanted to do was play basketball. He was often recruited to be a player for San Jacinto's team or for some other associations when there were leagues and competitions. That summer, he made it to a national competition when his local team sponsored by the Sugarcane Planters Association won. This was possibly the last time I saw him happy. I remember how excited he was when he found out that they were going to play in Capiz which required a trip he had never taken before, a three-hour bus ride from San Jacinto to Sugbu city, and from there a twelve-hour boat ride to Capiz where he and his team stayed for five days. Omar came home beaming with pride that their team came in second place and for days all he talked about was the trip. He said, "You know, for an hour I walked the streets on the last day of our trip, and it's really no different from San Jacinto, only a bit bigger and busier, and I asked myself if I could live there. I thought I could, but then when I came back to our motel, the first thing I did was pack my things. I missed home. On the boat ride, I kept looking at the clock, counted the hours, and I realized that I could not live anywhere else but here. You, on the other hand…" This conversation took place during a thirty-five minute walk to get to where we were that afternoon, sitting on a patch of grass in the far eastern end of the Benitez *hacienda*. That I was leaving in a week for the city loomed in my mind. I knew it was going to take a long time before Omar and I would walk the vast stretches of verdant land again and bask in its tranquility together. I gazed at the sugarcanes and the Narra trees as though I were quietly bidding them goodbye. I looked at Omar whose disposition had turned rather serious after the talk about home. I tried not to get into a sullen mood with my thoughts of departure, but, alas, I could not manage to be cheerful. I picked up a stone and threw it as far as I could. Omar stood up and wiped the dirt from his shorts then took out a pack of cigarettes from his pocket. I had been away for so long that I did not know he smoked. I tried smoking once when Don Rafael left half a cigarette in the ash tray. Omar offered me a cigarette and I smoked with him.

"What is it that you truly want in life, Benjamin?" He asked.

"I don't know. It's not just one thing. I guess I want to experience more of life. And for me that means I have to get away from here."

"Life here isn't good enough for you?"

"It's not that it isn't good enough. It's a vast world. I want to explore it. See what's out there. Of course San Jacinto will always be my home no matter where I will be."

"Do you swear on mama's grave that this will always be home to you?"

"Oh, don't be ridiculous. I don't have to swear. Where else would I consider home but here?"

"You never know. You might fall in love with another place and consider that place your home. People leave this place and never come back. That has happened."

"Well, I am sure that home is here, and I am sure that I will keep coming back especially if this is where I'd find you. Don't be such a doubter. You plan on staying here forever?"

"I don't know. I don't really plan. I just kinda go with the flow. And well, I don't really want to leave papa alone. I worry how he's gonna manage being alone. You know, I wouldn't mind if he met someone and remarried."

"I don't mind either. You remember when we were kids and women would come by and drop off some food or offer to help him? And papa ignored them."

"Maybe I should drop hints that it's okay for him to be with another woman. That way, papa can have some company. It's a normal thing to do. I'm sure mama in heaven wouldn't mind. You know he's gone back to drinking."

"Yeah, I noticed that. But that's not something to be overly concerned about, is it? We've seen him drink before with *tio* and their friends."

"I know but it's been occurring more frequently that it's become a habit. Just have to keep an eye on him. Well, I guess you'll be a city boy soon, eh?"

"Indeed. What about you, Omar? What is it that you want in life? Surely there must be something that you want."

"Sure."

"What?"

"A girl." He stood up and started walking away.

"Where are you going?"

"To see a girl. You once told me to go after what I want. Now that's what I'm going to do."

"You're going to leave me here to go after a girl? You have to go right this minute? Hey, which girl? Do I know her? I bet it's that girl with short hair I saw you flirting with the other night. What's her name? Sally? Soledad?"

"I'll tell you about it later."

He took off running so fast that I did not bother catching up with him. That was our last meaningful summer together. I walked back home relishing each step, in case, I thought, I wouldn't be able to walk those paths again. The sky turned amber in the approaching dusk and strangely lifted whatever gloom I had felt earlier. It was as if the death of the day held a certain promise, and I walked in the dark eager for the new life I was to embark on.

15

SOME NIGHTS WHEN I HAD a hard time sleeping in my room at Don Rafael's house, I would get up from my bed and go outside. Sometimes, I lay on the grass. It seemed as though I had never seen the world from that angle, as though the stars there were more brilliant, the grass lusher, the universe more receptive. Perhaps it was because I did not have to worry about what to eat the next day; because it felt good to sleep on a mattress that didn't hurt my back; because I had an old Adidas shoe box where I kept my savings. Sometimes, I said my bedtime prayers out there and believed that God heard me. On evenings when it rained, I went to the veranda and sat on Don Rafael's favorite chair, a large rattan piece with olive green cushions given to him by a friend who owned a furniture store in the city. I pretended to be a man of great stature and fine taste. I made gestures as though I were smoking a cigar and holding a glass of wine. I made up dialogues as if I were in the company of other equally prominent men, talking about the new beach house and holiday trips, and laughing in their wealthy sort of laugh. But it was when it rained that I missed papa and Omar the most so I sat there on those rainy nights beset with longing. I thought of specific things, the way Omar yawned or rubbed his right eye when he was sleepy, or his little fits of temper. I pictured the way papa stood by the open window and took a last glance at the world outside before he went to bed, or the way he scratched his head when he was thinking of something. I even thought of the big plastic bucket placed behind the door to catch the water falling from our leaking roof. In those rainy evenings I returned to bed teary-eyed with sentimentality and lay there wondering how they fared without me. If sleep did not come right away, I longed for papa's nighttime stories, so I would read a book hoping it would help me fall asleep.

I rose at six in the morning on week days. After I showered, I went to the kitchen where *Manang* Lita had already prepared breakfast for us servants. We often had rice, sardines, and scrambled eggs with onions and tomatoes. On weekends, instead of fish and scrambled eggs, we had corned beef paired with either chorizo or *tocino*. For merienda, we had fried bananas and soft drinks. *Manang* Lita forced me to eat when I did not have any appetite, remarking that I needed to gain at least ten pounds. When she heard me coughing, she boiled ginger root and let me drink it twice a day every day until the cough was completely gone. When I was feverish, she let me stay in bed and wrapped me in blankets so I would sweat and make the fever go away. She had a natural motherly instinct and perhaps, when she found out that mama had passed away years ago, she became doubly maternal. I too became protective of her.

One morning when I woke up earlier than usual and went straight to the kitchen, I was surprised to see her sitting there. When she became aware of my presence, she immediately stood up, put her hands to her eyes as if wiping away tears. She went to the sink and washed her face. It was unlike her not to acknowledge my presence. Though tap water was running, I heard her sniffle which then made me suspect that she had been crying. She asked me why I was up early. "I don't know," I said. It was true, I myself wondered why I woke up at five fifteen in the morning.

"You were crying before I came in," I said.

"What? No, just a cold. It's nothing. It's nothing."

Her mood the whole day was noticeably different. But it was not "nothing," for some time in the evening when she complained of a stomach ache and retired to bed early, I overheard *Manang* Ines and *Manang* Perla talk about what was the matter.

"It's that goddamn husband of hers. That good-for-nothing degenerate of a man."

"The nerve to have another mistress when he could not even sustain a job. And who is this loose woman he is running off with this time?"

"Many times I told her to leave him. Screw this machismo nonsense. Who needs a husband like that? He's nothing but a burden to her. I haven't had a husband in twenty-five years and my life is peaceful," said *Manang* Perla, strong and feisty at age sixty-two.

"Well, you didn't leave your husband, Perla. He died. You didn't really have a choice."

"Well, I didn't get another one, did I?"

"Maybe she stays for Carlos' sake."

"Carlos is fifteen, old enough to understand. Besides, he knows what his father is like because that bastard is shameless, indiscreet. He parades her for everyone to see."

"Poor boy. And poor Lita. All the money she's earning is just going to the booze and the *kabit*."

It was then that I found out that Rogelio, her husband, was a drunkard and a womanizer. He could not keep a job because he was lazy, disruptive, and had a habit of leaving his work post to go for a *cerveza*. There had been many occasions when he was asked to leave an establishment for being rowdy. He was also the type of man who bullied or threatened a woman. When he demanded money from *Manang* Lita, she readily gave it to him without putting up a fight. And typical of that kind of man, he knew how to manipulate her. Whenever she went home for a weekend visit, he cooked her meals, picked red roses from someone's backyard and handed it to her the moment she walked in their front door. "How's my beautiful wife, my one and only, my one true love," he would say.

Stories about his infidelities and drunken stupors reached *Manang* Lita through gossip. She refused to believe them until one day Carlos told her that he saw a younger woman sitting on his father's lap at Isko's *carenderia* at two in the afternoon when he should have been at work. On his own, Carlos left their home to live with his grandmother, *Manang* Lita's mother. Since Carlos' revelation about Rogelio, *Manang* Lita refused to go to the town market to avoid being the subject of gossip and ridicule. Before my arrival in the household, she asked either *Manang* Ines or *Manang* Perla to go to the market for her. Or she made a list for *Manong* Ramon whenever he went to town. The marketing task was then passed on to me. The five of us were like family. Even *Manong* Ramon who had a distant way about him could be counted on for anything. That was not to be the only time I witnessed *Manang* Lita's tears for there were many, many days like that and all for the same reason.

One night when I heard her coughing, and I brought ginger tea to her room. She lay on her side facing the open window, both her hands under her left cheek. A candle flickered in the dark. Her face was lit by the full moon that night.

And it is still clear in my mind now: her swollen eyes, the lines on her forehead. It was the face of a good woman, tired, and broken over the years. She asked me to come closer to her, so I sat on the bed. She said that I was a good child, that my mama in heaven would be proud of me. She hoped that the goodness in me would be carried over throughout my adulthood, that I should strive to always be a righteous person. "And treat your woman right. You know, when you have a girlfriend or a wife, do not be like Rogelio." She was teary-eyed again and told me to leave her alone now as she had to pray the rosary. I left her room and went to mine tired and sad and made a promise to myself that I would never treat a woman the way *Manang* Lita was treated by Rogelio.

By the time I moved to the city and began attending the university, I had lost contact with her. I did not even get to see her before I left for Los Angeles. So it was both a shock and a joy when I saw her at papa's wake. I whisked her away to a quiet area and we talked for hours. She said she lived with Carlos' family now since Rogelio passed away. Good riddance, I thought, for I blamed Rogelio for all her sorrows. She said her life was now about her grandchildren, two boys and two girls. How glad I was that there was no more sadness in her eyes. She asked about my life in Los Angeles. "No wife yet?" "Girl-friend?" "What kind of work do you do?" "I always knew you were going to make it big someday, son. Never had a doubt. I am proud of what you have made for yourself."

I did not say much about my life except in general terms, the nature of my work, how close I was to Hollywood, that yes, there was a woman in my life. Townsfolk have a mis-conception about people like me who live and work abroad, that life is all prosperity devoid of tribulations. I said nothing of my struggles for they were mild compared to hers, or to anyone there for that matter. Besides, I cared more about listening to her describe her present condition. She informed me that *Manang* Perla passed away five years ago, feisty and loud-mouthed to the very end. *Manang* Ines moved to another city to live with her daughter. Images of those early years in Don Rafael's house kept appearing in my head so that I was only partially listening to her and partially reminiscing, and in doing so, I seemed to appear somewhat distracted or lost in thought that she asked if I was tired or had she kept me from attending to other tasks. I told her it was none of those, that I was merely happy to see her again. When it was time for her to leave, she told me that she said a novena for papa. "May he rest in peace, and to you, dear child, you are always in my prayers."

I held her hands and took one good look at her, suddenly sad at the thought that I may not see her again. We walked to the main road where a tricycle was waiting for her. And during this short walk, it was as if I walked with her the way we used to do on some nights many years ago when she needed some air and asked me to accompany her. During those walks, she put her arm around my shoulder and was mostly quiet as though there were things on her mind. I remembered how the quiet was broken by a deep breath or a sigh and every time this happened, I glanced at her, wondering what she was thinking about, but I was too timid to ask. I realized then that adults were always preoccupied with serious matters, and I was relieved I had none of their grave predicaments.

"Well, I can walk myself from here. Listen, Benjamin, you've turned out to be a very fine man. You have made your papa very proud, I am sure of this. May God bless you always and may you continue to walk the path to righteousness. Now go."

I embraced her and left as told. When I rejoined the crowd, I scanned everyone's faces and looked back at my memory of each one of them no matter how small or inconsequential or vague. I paid attention to the elders' conversations; some were philosophical, others were merry, and some were sentimental. Histories were recounted, wars, what the country was like during their time. There were many recollections of moments when they were nine or seventeen or twenty-five, before the construction of the housing projects, when they swam in the river at night. Each had his own story to tell of those bygone years as if the past was all they had left to talk about. And as I sat there quietly listening to papa's friends and comrades, it seemed as though I walked into his life before I was born. Images of him as a child, as a teen, then as man in his early twenties flashed before me. A sudden drizzle slowly dissipated the crowd and around a little past midnight, everyone had left. I stayed up for another hour putting things away, empty bottles and leftover food. Omar was nowhere to be found. I slept in the veranda glad of the smell of air infused with rain. I thought of papa in his younger days in the way his friends spoke of him, how he had never angered anyone or said anything to provoke ill will. From them I also learned that papa was an inquisitive, bright child whose dream was to become a history teacher. I was in a dreamlike state and I felt a strange sense of lightness as I lay outside, papa and I finally home.

16

AFTER I GOT THE RENTAL CAR from the auto shop, I drove home and chanced upon *Tio* Andres. I immediately stepped on the car breaks upon seeing him. He looked thinner, his hair all gray. I honked to catch his attention, and he turned around to check where the sound came from. Something about his astounded gaze when he turned to look made me recall the many faces of his I've seen over the years, the wonderful man whom I looked up to like a father. He was there the very first time I opened my eyes to this world, when I let out my first cry and uttered my first word. He was there when I was learning to walk, when I first bruised my knee from a fall. He was there when Omar was born, and shed tears of joy and sorrow when birth and death arrived on the same evening. He witnessed Omar's moods and peculiarities, and it always seemed to me that he knew my brother in a way that I did not, thus there was a special bond between them. He was there at every milestone of our lives, all moments of splendor, shock, and turmoil. Above all, he was there for papa as a confidant, as his best friend. Seeing him again warmed my heart as though I was a lost child waiting to be found, and seeing him from afar was an affirmation that I was found and would soon be brought home.

"*Tio* Andres!" I yelled when I got out of the car. A look of surprise and delight showed in his face when he recognized me. I opened the trunk and took out the packages that I brought for them. For *Tio* Andres, a carton of Marlboro red, a dozen shirts I got from a shop along Hollywood Boulevard, a Lakers cap, a pair of sunglasses, two pairs of rubber shoes. I did not know what was in the bag for *Tia* Gloria as Cora was the one who had put it all together.

He ran towards me and gave me a hug.

"I'm so glad to see you, son. Gloria and I knew you were arriving any day now. She even guessed that you were going to arrive today. And here you are. Did you just get here? Just now?"

"This morning, but I got a flat tire as I was making a turn at the corner of the Miranda pharmacy. I was so glad there's an auto shop nearby, so I waited until it got fixed. Here, I brought some goodies for the family. How is everyone?"

"Thank you so much. You didn't have to bring us all these *pasalubong* but thank you. Gloria will really be happy. She is out doing laundry for the Martinezes. You still remember them? A lot of new people in town. More work for her, which is good for us, I suppose. But she complains of back pains and arthritis and then I have to massage her almost every night before she goes to sleep, and I tell her not to take on so much work but she's stubborn. Your *tia* has always been a stubborn woman. Jose, Arturo, and Claudia have all moved to where their spouses are from. Maybe your *Tia* Gloria's constant meddling and nagging drove them nuts. Or maybe they got tired of living here all their lives. You young people easily get bored."

"Well, look at me. I stayed as far away as possible."

"I always knew you were not meant to live here forever. When you were a kid you were always talking about this place and that, and this thing and that, and you would ramble about things that other kids your age never thought or talked about. Destiny, you know. You can't control your destiny."

I was surprised at what he said, and if the circumstance of my homecoming was different, I would have pressed further. What else was I like as a kid? And destiny? What about that?

"You must be tired, son. How about some fresh cocoa? You want to come inside or do you want to sit over there?" He pointed to the table and *kawayan* bench by the banana tree.

"I missed your cocoa, *Tio* Andres, and I really wish you had some the moment I saw you. I think I'll stay out here and enjoy the sun. I missed the air out here too, it's like no other. The smell of home."

"Okay, I'll be right back with *pandesal*. You're just in time for *merienda*."

I sat on the bench and surveyed the place. I remembered how my brother and I spent many nights here after an afternoon of play with Jose, Arturo, and Claudia. In the morning, we all had cocoa and *pandesal* for breakfast. We all managed to fit in their tiny space, packed together like a can of sardines, which, as children of poor farm workers, was something we were used to, and even found fun.

Tio Andres came out and brought me a mug filled with hot cocoa and six pieces of *pandesal*. "You must miss these *pandesals*. Do they have them in America?"

"Yes, but it's not the same."

I dipped the *pandesal* into the cocoa then I took a big bite. My thoughts remained on those bygone days where right on that same ground the five of us would stand with our thin weary legs, playing, laughing, teasing each other to the point of tears. An image of my brother hiding behind those far-off bushes briefly appeared, and even the way he laughed when he was found was so clear in my head. Old memories paraded before me: myself as a child, closing my eyes when we played hide and seek, how I did not really count from one to ten but instead tried to listen intently to the sound of their footsteps to get a sense of the direction in which they were heading; how they would accuse me of cheating by pretending that I'd closed my eyes, when in fact, I did not and was looking at where they headed off to hide. I drifted as I remembered it all, and for a moment I forgot that I was Benjamin who had just arrived there that day to collect his brother's ashes, failing to hear what *Tio* Andres was saying to me while my mind wandered.

"Benjamin?"

"Huh? Sorry, *tio*. I got distracted about something."

"You were. You must be tired. Perhaps you should rest. We have a lot to talk about but I do not have enough time right now so we'll have to speak later. I will come see you tonight. I have some carpentry work in town. I was about to head out when you saw me. I have to leave now before it gets dark. How long are you staying?"

"I will be here for about two weeks. Thought I'd use the extra days to drive down south. I've never been there. Okay, *tio*, I will be expecting you tonight."

"Benjamin, your brother's ashes are in your room. Your *tia* thought that it was best to keep it there. And there is a box or two full of his stuff. I did not go through the contents. Oh, here are the keys to the house and to your room. Your *tia* cleaned it last week. Everything should be in order."

"About Omar—well, I guess we'll talk later. Thank you, *tio*. Will *tia* be coming with you tonight?"

"I'm afraid not. I prefer to see you alone tonight. Besides, she will be tired and whiny and complain about her body pains. But before I go, I want to ask you if you heard about Don Rafael."

"No. What about?"

It was then that he told me about the storm, how everyone in town was waiting to hear whether he was alive or dead. The storm occurred while I was on the plane, on my way to Sugbu.

"And there had been talks going around for a while now that he is being investigated," he added.

"Investigated for what?"

"I don't know the particulars. But word is that it is something criminal or illegal. I was not shocked. You see, karma spares no one. Not even the powerful and wealthy. I thought you might have heard about this."

"No. The last time he and I spoke was a few months ago. It was very brief. He called and asked me for a favor. He wanted me to contact his niece in Northern California and ask for her address."

"I know that you have a lot of respect for him. A lot of gratitude and it's understandable. But he was a heartless bastard. A piece of scum, the worst kind. The worst kind."

The first time I saw *Tio* Andres get upset was when I was about nine years old. He scolded Jose for pushing his younger brother, Arturo, over a trivial argument they both had. *Tio* smacked Jose in the head, fiercely admonishing him not to hurt his brother like that again, and sent him off to do a chore. The second time happened during an evening of drinking with his *compadres* at his house. He raised his voice to the point of screaming that made everyone get quiet. As I grew older, I came to realize that there were things that ignited his sensibilities, things that have to do with his beliefs and principles in life.

"What are you upset about, *tio*? And what are you saying about Don Rafael?"

"We will talk about it later tonight. I am sorry I got carried away. Forgive me. I still have a hard time talking about Omar. I do not even know where to begin. And I know it is harder on your part to comprehend everything that happened. My apologies. Well, I have to leave now."

We walked quietly towards the main road. He gave me a hug before we parted ways. It was the sort of embrace a father would give to a son after a period of long absence, unabashed, full of good feeling that he was home. With a heavy heart, I got inside my car and drove off to the house.

17

AFTER PARTING WITH *TIO* ANDRES, the afternoon that had
been cast with streaks of gold lost its shimmer. When I stood
in front of the house, I felt no attachment to it, not even a sense
of pride that building this house was once a dream of long
ago and now I have fulfilled it. To call home a house that was
unfamiliar to me, to have arrived at the cold fact of opening
the front door where my brother's ashes awaited me reduced
me to despair. I stood there for a moment, hesitant to reach
for the doorknob. I lit a cigarette and went back to the car to
grab the liquor. I walked around trying to remember if Omar
gave instructions of what to do with his ashes. Did he want
them scattered in the sea? Did he want them spread all over
the land that had held his footsteps? Or did he leave it to my
own choosing? Once more, I contemplated the last night of
his life, what his thoughts were before sleep finally came, if
it came at all, how he spent the hours while waiting for the
moment, that final moment when he became completely free
from the weight of this world. I took a gulp from the bottle of
rum and headed straight for the door.

It was cold and quiet inside, eerily quiet as though the
objects and furniture were left to care for the house in the
absence of its occupants. It was tidy, just as I expected, but had
it been unkempt or vandalized, it would not have mattered to

me. On the second floor was a small table with framed photos of the three of us. I wondered if Omar was the one who placed them there. There was a photo of us sitting next to each other, smiling, holding a glass, and making a toast to something—Good health! Togetherness! Life!—all of it.

That same image had been etched in my memory for that took place on the first evening of my very first homecoming since I'd moved to Los Angeles. Whenever I felt homesick, I often thought of that night, and of other nights like that, when laughter was good, when one felt as though nothing else in the world could equal that kind of happiness. I grabbed the frame and held it close to my heart. How strange the way death glorifies—He was a great man; I cannot forget his kindness; He had no mean bone in his body—and also reduces one to a mere photograph or ashes in a jar languishing quietly in a room that means nothing to you. I tried to feel both of these things, but the more I tried, the more their absence was magnified. I put back the frame on the table and headed to my room.

Omar had picked that room to be mine because it had the biggest window. He said I had a thing for windows. When I opened the door, I instantly saw Omar's ashes for it sat on the shelf directly across the door. Shock flowed through every vein in my body. It all seemed so final, irretrievable—his absence. Shaking, I took the jar and held it with both hands, delicately, sorrowfully. I held it in the way I held Omar when I carried him in my arms as a baby and put him to sleep. Two large brown boxes beside the book shelf caught my attention. I put the jar back on the shelf and rummaged through the boxes. One box contained posters of various bands, two song books, and a stack of old newspapers. The other box contained some

notebooks, letters, and postcards that I'd sent over the years.
I leafed through the pages of the notebook.

> I used to go by the river
> And watch the dead leaves
> And wooden twigs float down
> Or the way the water shimmered
> Against the April sun
> I went there for peace
> For nothingness
> And sometimes cry the tears
> Of a harrowed life, of luck running out
> Or just tears for an overwhelming sense
> Of not knowing, not understanding

My brother, the poet. Why I had never been aware of his
propensity for the written word, I blame myself entirely.

> It is the way
> Your light trickles
> Like moonbeams
> When you sleep
> That makes the flowers
> Alive at night
> Even they are vivified
> At your wonderment
> It is you
> Who makes the world
> Propel some sort of music
> And euphonic hosannas
> Swirl through the expanse

Then one solid melody
Descends from the sky
And this is when
The earth flaunts her motley blooms
And the birds resume their lyrical world
Because of this
I cancel all thoughts
Of a fallen world
Of myself feeling helpless
Among the living
It is you who makes this life
So welcoming, so purposeful
You, constant flare of my heart
The singular beat
That does not falter
I give back to you
And to the world
Everything that you have turned beautiful.

There was a shoe box inside that contained letters. From
the yellow and purple envelopes, it was apparent that they were
from a woman. I looked closely at the first three envelopes in
the stack, and indeed, the sender's name was that of a woman.
It comforted me to think that perhaps there was someone,
perhaps that woman, whom he'd turned to for comfort and
who made him feel alive. I knew nothing of Omar's personal
relationships, knew nothing of him at all. I put the letters back
in the box, hesitant to read them afraid of what I might discover; for instance, his sadness of which I'd done nothing to
alleviate, or his grievances, for I imagined he bared his soul
to her and thus I presumed those letters were brimmed with

confessions. No, I was not ready at that moment to read the whole truth. Suddenly I had a compulsion to go to our old hut, to go *home*. I carried the jar with me.

The day began to fade away, at least it seemed that way to me as I walked towards the hut. If the allure of *gumamelas* and *santan* was present, it escaped my notice. When I was inside the hut, a smell of the past wafted by, something to do with molasses and dust and northern wind. I put Omar's ashes next to papa's old radio. Perhaps that radio will outlast us all. Over there, I said to myself, we squatted on the floor and ate food. Right there was where we placed our can of marbles. I opened the window and looked out into the world I'd left behind for America.

By now I was reduced to utter nostalgia, and I was at a loss of what to do with the ashes, or with my life, for that matter. Something fell from the altar above me. A leaf, a dead leaf from dead flowers inside a can of Milo. What fell and brushed against my skin was not just the leaf itself but also sadness. Everything fell wordlessly upon me, and all I could do was lay on the floor and curl in fetal position. And then I felt ashamed and disgusted at myself for not having shed any tears even at the home where we were once a family. "Damn you. Damn all of you! But also, forgive me. Forgive me, please," I screamed as though someone or something out there was behind all this misfortune but was also bestowed the sole power to absolve everything.

What do you know about suffering? I kept hearing this line in my head as I walked back to the house from the hut. It was half past six in the evening when I began drinking again for it seemed like there was nothing else to do while my life was on a standstill. What else was I to do? I put Omar's ashes back in my room. It felt to me as though I stirred his quiet there among the books, and he needed to be left alone again while I sort out the remainder of my broken life. Over time I had acquired a large collection of books. On weekends when I had nothing else to do, I went to garage sales and thrift stores and came home with a few paperbacks I bought for a dollar or two. I included books inside the *balikbayan* box that I sent three or four times a year. Besides thinking that any decent house should have a book shelf stacked with a good selection of books, I secretly wished that Omar took pleasure in reading them. I did not know if he ever took any interest until he mentioned it in one of his letters. It gave me pleasure to read that short line he wrote: Thank you for the books, I am enjoying them.

I tried not to overindulge with liquor so I'd remain coherent and lucid by the time *Tio* Andres came by later the evening. Then I began to despise the house. In my head, I took it apart down to its last plank of wood until the entire structure became non-existent. And it seemed as though I inhabited a vast stretch of emptiness until random movement outside made me look out the window, or a swish of air swayed the thin curtains and returned me to the sofa where I remained unmoved. Cora came to mind. I thought that I should give her a call or send an email. The thought of unpacking my things and charging electronic gadgets was daunting. Composing emails was a herculean task. Thoughts of papa took over. What did he have to say about all this? Was he watching over me as the spirits of loved ones were believed to do? I asked him to direct me to the path I should take now that they were all dead. I begged him to show up in whatever form, even his own ghost, looking down on me or sitting beside me, because he had all my attention now; I was home and ready to listen.

I stepped out the front door and looked around as though somewhere out there in the dark was a hidden message from my father's ghost. What was it that I failed to see all along? What gestures, intonations, silences had I discounted? I stood there in the quiet of night, attentive, but nothing happened, just the world going about its way, the moon and stars were present as usual, and the wind carried the muted cries of every mother, father, and child. I longed for typhoon number 4 to fall disastrously or for lightning to strike me. I even wished for a thief or a lunatic to attack me and leave me for dead. I went back inside and resumed drinking. My thoughts turned to Sisa, where and how to find her. I wanted to speak to her about the tragedy she foretold many years ago.

My emotional state left me so exhausted that I fell asleep on the sofa. I do not know how long I drifted but I was awakened by *Tio* Andres picking up a glass that fell on the rug. He said he hadn't been there long, only about ten minutes. He brought me food cooked by *Tia* Gloria, rice and *tinolang manok*, and he took the liberty of putting it in the kitchen. I thanked him and said I already ate, as I did not want to tell him that I had no appetite.

"Have it for breakfast or lunch then. Please eat. It will do you no good drinking like this on an empty stomach." He sat on the armchair across me and helped himself to a drink. The night deepened; the lizards made their usual squeaking sounds. An odd silence passed between us like we were strangers thrown together by chance, unsure of what to say to each other. I reached for a cigarette when he said, "Life was hard for your brother."

Life is hard for everyone, I thought; it certainly was for me as well. Of course people here would never think that way, especially if you are living abroad earning dollars. But what did they know about living in another country all on your own? What did they know about assimilation and adaptation? What did they know about the life of an immigrant and the struggles that come with it?

In my mind Omar's words to me returned: What do you know about suffering?

"Over the years he gradually became aloof, less sociable. He avoided his friends, stopped joining basketball leagues, stopped going to fiestas. After your papa died, he kept to himself almost completely. I welcomed those nights when he would pay me and Gloria a visit. I always told him to come back again tomorrow night and have dinner with us because I was worried about him. He paid us a visit when he felt like it. I suppose, he had a life of his own, and we respected that. We did not mind if he came over every night; we preferred that he did. When he came over, we'd have a drink, or he'd bring his guitar, and your *tia* and I would sing along. Your *tia* would give him food to take home. Did you know that he gained many fans from that guitar playing of his? He was a natural. At parties, people asked for him to provide some entertainment, but he stopped that also. Sometimes he did most of the talking; other times he didn't say much; he just asked me questions and listened to me ramble on."

A momentary calm stifled the discord in my head when I thought of Omar strumming his guitar with a sort of flair. His face looked peaceful, as though music dispelled the darkness in his soul. But what else was he doing in those solitary moments? What were his thoughts? How little I knew about him.

"He often brought up the past."

"Which part of the past?" I asked.

"Oh, those years of long ago when you were children running wild in these lands. He always brought it up. He'd say: 'I've never been happier than I was when we would just wander around all day, stumble upon new paths by getting lost.' He'd mention all the mischief you boys got into. How you'd purposely defy the No Trespassing signs on some *haciendas* and run as fast as you could when you were found out. He mentioned a time when you boys trespassed into Hacienda Luisa, how the caretaker—oh I know him, Gaudencio, an old cantankerous fool—yelled and approached you both, and in running away from him, Omar's right slipper broke so he ran all the way with just one slipper. He had the innocence of a child, but that same innocence also made him vulnerable, almost unfit for a harsh world. There was always a hint of sadness in his voice. And his eyes, too, seemed like they were always on the verge of tears. He wished you were around more, I think. He did not say it, but I can tell that he missed you. I think he may have confessed that to your *tia*. You both were very close when you were kids. He thought you were going to come back and live here again after your high school education. He didn't think that you would establish residence somewhere else. I remember when he was young, he kept waiting and waiting for you to come home."

"It hasn't always been easy for me being away, *tio*. I had my own struggles too from the very first time I left home up until I moved to Los Angeles. I had to learn to adjust to every place I lived, had to get acquainted with its people, its culture. I had a lot of learning and unlearning to do to survive. The struggle is private and internal, and perhaps others may dismiss it as a trifling matter. It is difficult for people to grasp this unless they have experienced it themselves. My sense of duty to provide for them was so strong that it motivated me to carry on. I consoled myself with the thought of us having a better life. Sometimes the one who leaves carries the weight more than the one being left behind. But one has to have left to know what this means. Now I wonder whether it was all worth it. I'm afraid it wasn't."

"Don't be hard on yourself, son. You did nothing wrong. You did what you had to do at that time. You were a child then."

"But I became an adult too. And I just carried on wherever life took me without any misgivings or resistance."

"It is your life that you have to live above all, and not how others want you to live it, not even your loved ones, even if they disapprove or misunderstand and cast judgment against you. Because if you don't follow what your heart tells you, you will end up with many regrets and that is not a good way to live. And you made it, Benjamin. Look at how far you've gone, what you achieved. You should be proud of yourself."

"I wish I knew what was going on inside him. If I did, perhaps things could have taken a different turn. I don't know if he told you, *tio*, that we had an argument one night during papa's wake. He said I was selfish, that nothing I did for them mattered. It seemed like he had been keeping those feelings for a long time and he could no longer hold them back, hence his outburst. I didn't understand his anger then, I still don't. It's not like I forged a new life for myself and abandoned them. I admit, for a long time, I was dismayed at his lack of ambition and his defeated attitude. I worked hard and sent money for his education, etcetera. I told him he could take up any course, or study in the city if he wanted. I told him he could come visit me anytime. But he refused everything I offered. So there came a point where I just gave up on him. *Tio*, did

Omar confide in you? Did he mention anything about what was bothering him?"

"He hated your papa's drinking. He didn't say it out loud, but I saw how difficult it was for him to witness Pablo slowly destroy himself like that, not caring about anything. Well, it was like seeing his slow demise. Oh, it was Pablo like I've never seen before. He drank more than he ate. Sometimes he didn't eat at all. It came to a point when Omar had to force him to eat. Pablo got into arguments with others, including random strangers. Nothing that escalated into something big, like a fistfight, but still, it was unlike him to have a spat with anyone. He passed out everywhere. Some of my friends who chanced upon him falling asleep on public benches took pity and took him home. Nobody wanted to be around him anymore."

"I don't understand why papa became an alcoholic. He didn't resort to heavy drinking after mama died. I thought that perhaps something must have happened to him, but I couldn't bring myself to ask him. I felt the strain on papa and Omar's relationship though neither one of them told me about it. It must have been difficult for Omar. Maybe that added to his resentment. I was not around so maybe he felt all alone."

"They had some disagreements like any other father and son would have. But there was one thing that caused the rift between them, the main cause for everything that happened."

By now the air carried the smell of impending rain. It was the very smell that made Omar and me run outside and stretch our arms wide under the sky, waiting for the first drop, standing there until it arrived. I remembered how we took off our shirts and let the rain glide over our bodies. I recalled how incomprehensible the joy was, the way we jumped and laughed as though we were little farmers thankful to the heavens for nourishing the soil. But the evening air also carried a whiff of gloom. It gave out a hint that peace would not come that night, and perhaps never again; that there lurking amidst the objects on the glass table, the works of art that gave color to the plain walls, among the accumulation of shiny things, also sat sorrow, silent, biding its time before it came out.

A sudden roar of thunder made *Tio* Andres and I look out the window, then at each other, trying to go back to where we were before each got lost in a moment of thought. Cigarette ashes were on the floor.

Tio Andres stood up, and suddenly he was in tears. He promptly turned away from me as if attempting to hide the water in his eyes. He walked towards the window and fumbled with the curtains. I must go to him, I thought. I should put my arm around his shoulder and console him. Rain began to fall. I let him alone looking out into the night as if he required a moment to summon the words he was about to tell me. His right hand rubbed his eyes, or wiped the tears away; I could not tell.

"Well," he said, his back still against me, "Pablo resorted to heavy drinking after you went away to live with Don Rafael. I thought perhaps he simply got lonely after you left and that it was just a phase. But it wasn't what I thought it was, far from it."

He turned to me and said, "There are things that you do not know, Benjamin. I stand before you, a torn man. Your papa carried a secret for many years and brought it with him to his grave. He made me swear not to tell anyone including you. I made a promise to him, and now I am about to break it.

"It is against my principle not to keep my word especially to your father who is a brother to me but in this case, and only in this situation do I make an exception. I will break my promise because I cannot bear to look you in the eye and not tell you the truth. You deserve to know the truth.

"One evening, Pablo and I were drinking outside your hut. It was very late. Omar had gone to bed hours before, so we thought he was asleep. You were already living at Don Rafael's at that time. Anyway, your papa got drunk, very drunk that he started crying without let-up. I have not seen him in that state before, not even when your mama died. I asked him what was the matter. He said he needed to confess something otherwise he would go mad. He made me promise not to tell anyone. Things were never the same again since that night. I believe that it had an impact on your brother all throughout his life."

"What about that night, *Tio* Andres? What happened that night?"

18

"I CANNOT LIVE WITH MYSELF, Andres. I have done something horrible. A terrible, terrible sin. I am going to hell. I am in hell. You have no idea about the demons I have. I cannot bear it any longer."

"What are you talking about, Pablo? Sin? What sin? What could you have possibly done? You are drunk and talking nonsense but that is not a sin, is it? I don't believe you broke any laws or the ten commandments with your drunken state, but Padre Ramon might give you a harsh scolding."

"But I had no choice, Andres, I had to do it. You must understand why I had to do it."

"Do what? What did you do? You are not making any sense. I don't know if I should listen to this nonsense while you are drunk."

"Andres, please listen to me. I know I am drunk, but my mind is still intact. Please believe me. What I am about to tell you is a gravely serious matter. You are the only one I trust in this world. But forgive me because once I tell you, it will become your burden too.

"It is okay, Pablo. Talk to me. What have we not gone through together in our lives? You are like a brother to me. Your sons are my sons, as my children are yours. If the burden should be mine too, then so be it. Tell me what happened. I am listening."

"You see, I approached Don Rafael and asked him if I can work on weekends at his *hacienda* in Argon for I needed extra money. Benjamin has been begging me about him going to school. Every night before he sleeps, that's all he talks about. He even said that he will work long hours at the hacienda just to save up money to help pay for expenses. But I would not allow him to work. Besides, there's Omar to be watched over and taken care of. Poor Benjamin and his dreams. Those were my hopes for myself as a child, and I wish for him the same thing. I have always felt sorry for the boys that they were deprived of having a mother. I felt that they deserved something a little better in life because of their loss. Hearing Benjamin plead breaks my heart. I could not deny this to him. Even a year or two of schooling is still education, isn't it? Don't we want our children to have better lives than the ones we had? I want him to experience what it's like to sit in a classroom, have classmates, learn to read and write, be a little literate and educated. It is what he desires."

"I understand your sentiments and agree with all of them, Pablo. What did Don Rafael say?"

"He said he'll see what he can do, that it can be arranged. Then I let it alone, having brought it up with him already. But one morning, he pulled me aside and said that we needed to talk privately about what I had asked him. He asked me to come to his house around three and have *merienda* with him. I was very nervous, Andres. I've never sat with him, let alone have *merienda* in his home. He said, "I know you want your son to go to school. I respect that a lot. I respect you for it. Education is important to get ahead in this world. The youth get into a lot of mischief these days. Drugs, especially. You know I can help you. And I will. In fact, I will take care of your son's future. All the way to the very end. He can go to any university that he chooses, take any course he wants. His future is secured, you have my word. Do you trust me, Pablo?"

"Of course, I trust you, Don Rafael." I assured him. "I was only thinking a year or two in elementary school, let him experience it then see what happens next. I am thankful for your generous offer. But I don't know how I can ever repay you. All our lives and my forefathers before me, we worked at your hacienda, did what we were told, served you with all our heart. You've always had our loyalty and gratitude, and forever it shall be that way. And that is all a man such as myself can do and offer. No matter how long I live, I can never fully repay the money that you will have spent on my son for an education in the university."

"Ah, but you insult me, Pablo. I do not want your money."

"Forgive me, I did not mean to insult you. I would never do that to you, Don Rafael."

"You know, I still remember the very first time I saw you, Pablo. We were kids then. It is remarkable the things one remembers. You sat on the bench under the acacia tree. That tree still stands. Feel free to take a look later if you want to refresh your memory. Do you remember that day? I was observing you from my bedroom window, and was eager to come down and join you, but, you know, my nanny at that time had me follow rigid rituals of taking a bath and eating breakfast, so on. After I had finished, I came out looking for you, but you were gone. I wanted to invite you to come inside the house and show you my toys. But what I remember distinctly above all that day, and this may sound strange to you, was that I had a good feeling about you. Does that ever happen to you? You know, when you hardly know someone, yet you just have this feeling that that person is trustworthy or that your paths will cross again. You're a good man, Pablo. An honorable man as your father was. My own father thought your father was a good man. I know every man in this town. I know what they are like, their families, their history, their debts, their indiscretions and infidelities. I know men's mistresses and their rendezvous. I know that your wife passed away giving birth to your second son. It must be hard bringing up two boys on your own, though we are fortunate that, if you are familiar with the phrase 'it takes a village to raise a child', ours is one of those remaining places that abide by such a belief. And thank God for that. Well. If you are really serious about your son going to school, this is your chance. I only offer once. However, there is something I do ask from you in return. And I ask you only because I trust you. Do you know how many people before you have come asking me the very same thing that you ask of me? But a man can only do so much. I cannot save the world, but I will help those who deserve it. You and your family, Pablo, are one of those few, deserving people."

"I will do anything for my sons, Don Rafael. And I will do anything to repay the kindness that you have bestowed on me."

"Very well, then. What is today? *Miercoles? Viernes a las nueve de la mañana*, I will pick you up at your house. Expect to be back at home for late evening. It is probably best not to let your sons wait up for you."

"What happened then, Pablo? Did he pick you up like he said? Jesus! Jesus! I am getting very nervous right now."

"Yes, he picked me up. Everything happened so fast, Andres. I did not even have time to contemplate. Besides, do you suppose I could have said no to him? That I could have refused, and then walk away just like that? You know what happens to people who disappoint him. Besides, he owns the land that gives us work, our hut sits on his land. Where would we to go if he fired me or ordered us to leave his land? Anyway, we drove south. I am not familiar with the south, not past Carmen. We drove another two hours past Carmen. And it was at this point that things started to become strange.

"Strange? What do you mean by that?"

"He pulled over and told me that I had to be blindfolded. And he did just that. It was then I knew something bad was going to happen."

"What? He blindfolded you? What was his explanation? What was your conversation in the car?"

"Before I was blindfolded, it was a pleasant drive. He seemed to be in deep thought. He smoked non-stop. Every now and then he'd ask about Benjamin, what he was like. He talked about how he'd always wanted a son. Then he'd talk a bit about politics, how it is such a dirty business. He talked about the south. They owned properties there. Then he said that we were nearing our destination and that's when he pulled over and blindfolded me. He said it had to be done because it was easier if I did not know the surroundings. He said it was best that he did not talk about what was going to transpire, that I would know about it once we arrived at our destination. I did not speak when he said I was to be blindfolded. I was too shocked and nervous to react. My shirt was damp with sweat. My hands were very cold. Finally, we stopped. He helped me get out of the car and held my hand as we walked. It was a bit of a walk. Then we finally stopped and he told me to wait, to not move from where I was standing. He told me not to speak at all. It was very quiet. Then we walked a bit more. It was a flat, open, grassy land that we walked on. Probably one of his properties. Then he said, "There are people who should not live in this world, Pablo. People who don't deserve to breathe the air that you and I breathe. Men who are traitors, for example. And sometimes we have to make a difficult decision to get rid of them for the sake of everyone." Next thing I knew, Don Rafael put something in my hand to hold. It was a gun. I had a gun in my hand and he positioned it in the way that my fingers were ready to pull the trigger. He raised my arm as if to aim the gun at someone. He held my arm steady as I was shaking. We took about three steps forward until I felt the tip of the gun touch what I knew was someone's head. But I did not hear any sound coming from this person. Maybe he was tied to a chair and his mouth was taped. And then Don Rafael told me to pull the trigger. Of course, I couldn't do it. I started crying. I couldn't stop crying. I wanted to shoot myself instead. Then he kept on talking about the boys, how as soon as tomorrow, they would not have to worry about our wretched lives. He reminded me of our conversation that one morning when he pulled me aside, that we had come to an agreement and that I had made a promise to him. He assured me that I would not be in trouble, that no one would harm or touch my family. And then he started yelling, "Pull the trigger! Shoot! Shoot!" his voice getting louder each time. He was getting impatient with me. I kept repeating in my head, God, please save me, God, send me a miracle, God forgive me, while Don Rafael kept yelling "Shoot now! Do it!" I feared what he would do to me. And so I did! I pulled the trigger and shot the person. I murdered someone, Andres! Then after that one shot, he let go of my arm and took the gun. I heard a loud thump. Then we walked back to the car. He held my arm throughout the walk. I was shaking. No word was spoken during our drive back.

I didn't know where we were when he took the blindfold off. I was not paying attention to the surroundings. I could only think of the person I killed. Tears fell from my eyes the entire time. He let me stay at his house to rest for a while. He said I needed to relax, that I had nothing to worry about, that everything would be fine. He reminded me again of our agreement, how my sons would now have better lives, how he would take care of their futures. He gave me some whisky and I drank it all in one gulp. I got home very late that evening. The boys were asleep. The next day, he indeed summoned Benjamin to come live at his house and made preparations for his schooling. He made true his promise. That is what happened, Andres. That is the sin I committed. This is why I stopped hearing Mass. I cannot stand my own existence. Do you understand why I might as well be dead already? There were so many times that I wanted to die, but I worry about the boys, and every morning when I wake up, I try my best to think about them so I have a reason to go on living. Please, Andres, I ask you to watch over them when I am gone. Forgive me. May God forgive my soul."

"Oh my god, Pablo, what have you done? Yes, we love our children, and we would do anything for them the best we can. But murder? Murder! A mortal sin! But I know you had no other choice at that moment, Pablo. You could not run. You could not say no to Don Rafael. No one can. Even if you said no, he would have silenced you for being privy to that crime. But what can we do now but pray to God and ask for forgiveness."

"Now do you understand my demons, Andres? This is why I drink. It makes me forget. But at least my sons will live well, that is all that matters to me. Benjamin is going to be an outstanding student. My boy's going to be successful someday, I just know it. When I am gone, I am confident he will take care of his brother just as he had always done. Do we have any more alcohol? Pour me another glass, my dear brother. Drown my sorrow with another drink."

"I can only imagine how difficult this is for you, but you are still alive Pablo, and you have a young son here that needs a father who is attentive and one who isn't always drinking. Children feel and notice everything. You've had enough drink for the night. Your problem will not go away by having another drink."

"Did you listen to what I just confessed to you? All I hear is the sound of the gun. Do you know what it's like to murder someone? No, you don't know, Andres, and you never will. Do you know that it haunts your thoughts first thing in the morning, all throughout the day until you sleep at night? It fills my spirit with indescribable anguish. I have nightmares. Sometimes I dream that I am walking, and a group of people approach me, and they yell to my face Murderer! Murderer! Or I dream of a faceless man tied to a chair and I see myself pointing a gun at his head. I killed a man, Andres. He could have been one of us. A father, maybe. An ordinary person who provoked Don Rafael's ire. A person who didn't deserve to die like that. And somewhere there is a family grieving, a widowed wife, orphaned children, and it is all because of my own doing. So damn everything else in this world because I want another drink. Indulge me, Andres. Just tonight, indulge me."

"Hush, Pablo. Be quiet. Omar is awake. Jesus, he must have heard. ..."

"Papa! Papa!"

"What are you doing standing there by the door? Go back to sleep, Omar. Stop crying and go back to sleep. Stop crying, I said."

"Papa! Papa!"

19

I CANNOT THINK ABOUT IT without going mad. It is hard to look at the world with the same pair of eyes, or to be the same man and abide by the same principle of being after that revelation. I remember that evening, the evening of my father's tears, one summer when I was nine. Omar and I were to sleep at *Tio* Andres and *Tia* Gloria's house. Omar and I did not mind as we spent the afternoon playing with our cousins, and we loved spending time with them. But as the night deepened, I felt restless, and I begged *Tia* Gloria to allow us to go home. She said that it was too late to be walking outside. I said that it was only quarter to nine, that papa would have no objections to us being out at night if we got home at ten sharp. This was not true, but I made it up out of desperation. *Tia* Gloria ignored me and continued sewing a pair of torn socks. I begged her to the point of tears so she finally gave in out of annoyance as I wouldn't shut up. She looked at *Tio* Andres for approval, and he scratched his head as though undecided about what to do with us. Before I could plead with him, he stood up and said he would walk us home. He took his bicycle so he could ride it on his way back to his house. When we started walking, he asked if I was not feeling well, that he had not seen me so desperate to go home. "I just want to go home, *tio*," I said. I myself could not give a reason for my restlessness.

"You promise me that you and Omar will stay indoors and go straight to bed. No foolishness, you hear?"

"I promise, *tio*."

"Don't wait up for your papa."

When we arrived home, Omar and I immediately went to lie down, and in a matter of minutes, he fell asleep. I was anxious and stared at the altar. There were statues of Santo Niño and Virgin Mary, and a large crucifix. Papa always told us to pray before going to sleep, and as I thought about praying, papa flung the door open, and perhaps realizing that we were there, he suddenly tiptoed his way to his bed. I pretended to be asleep for fear of being reprimanded for still being awake, or for coming home against his instructions. Then I heard a whimper coming from his makeshift room. At first I thought it was a noise from outside, as there was some commotion from people walking home from a nearby fiesta. As the crowd passed along and their voices were no longer audible, I heard it again and again, long into the deep night. First, a sniffle, then a sporadic, muffled sob. Curled up on the living room floor and sleepless, I listened intently and tried not to move. What does a boy of nine know about the affairs of the world that could drive his father to tears? What predicament could have warranted his sobs? With a fretful heart, I said a silent prayer asking God to bless papa. Then Omar tapped my shoulder. I slowly turned and motioned him to be quiet. Moonlight slipped through the spaces between the windows and lit our inquiring faces. I wanted to tell Omar to go back to sleep but I did not want papa to know that we were awake. I closed my eyes and pretended to sleep so Omar would sleep too. That night, Omar and I slept holding each other's hand.

In the morning papa woke me and told me that I had been summoned by Don Rafael. Still shaken by last night's incident,

I moved languidly and did not want to leave. But what choice did I have that morning, in that passive town, in the life that I was born into? Papa did not look at me as he gathered my things and put them in a plastic bag. "In case you have to stay there longer. Besides, I just noticed that Omar is coughing. I don't want you to get sick," he said with his back against me. He told me to eat the *pandesal* on the table so I could leave soon. I got up and went quietly to the kitchen. Omar was still asleep, and I did not want to disturb him. I ate hurriedly and stepped out. Papa was outside smoking a cigarette. Since when did he start smoking?

"I will come visit you in a few weeks," he said.

"Visit? How long am I to stay there?"

"We don't know how long Don Rafael wants you there. Be grateful. Any boy in this town would want to be in your shoes. And save the money that you earn," he said.

"I will, papa."

I recall the morning light that fell upon our nipa roof. A flock of birds glided against the sky. It was May, the height of summer. On both sides of the road, hectares of greenery woke up from last night's blackness. Lush with the blaze from the morning sun, the sugar canes seemed taller in my eyes. The stems that looked like bamboo were thicker; the leaves bent back and forth and played with the stray wind. It was the kind of morning that I loved waking up to as a child. Papa's eyes were moist and reddish. I became anxious and sensed that he was keeping something from me, or that something had transpired and left him in distress. I looked aside to stifle my own emotions. He came closer and gently pressed my right cheek with a hand that was so warm. Then he caressed my head and fixed my hair in a sort of gesture that seemed like he was getting me ready for something momentous. Our faces became level as he knelt before me and put his hands on my shoulders. He gave me a look that he had not given me before, as if his eyes betrayed him, and said *Farewell, my boy, and fare well in the world out there.* I stood waiting to hear some explanation about my sudden departure from home, or some confession about last night's tears, but no words came out of him, only a deep inhalation that was suspended for a moment, as though the universe had been sucked in, until finally, he breathed out warm air into my face. He gave me a hug and said that I should get going, that I should behave and follow, without any fuss or objection, what Don Rafael told me to do. I nodded. He stood up and cast a far-off stare into the expanse as if something had just caught his attention, a fleeting image, perhaps, or a pressing matter that he suddenly remembered. What troubled him that made him behave so strangely that morning? By then the shimmer of summer gold extended amply over the edges from where we stood as I thought of what to say to my father.

"Tell Omar I hid his marbles under the mango tree. I am going now, papa. I look forward to your visit."

"Okay, son. Take care now. Be good. I will see you soon."

"Goodbye, papa."

"Goodbye, son."

Off I went, restless and resigned. I had to get to the town square, a kilometer and a half from home, in my torn slippers, where a blue Toyota pick-up truck parked by the market entrance was waiting to take me to Don Rafael's house. I kept looking back until our hut was out of sight. I walked leisurely, counted my steps along the potholed road. I began to feel the dirt on my feet, the sweat from my forehead, the flutter of my ambivalent heart. To tell the truth, I became excited at the prospect of staying at Don Rafael's house. I welcomed the respite inside his palatial home, a proper cot to sleep on, and money that I can save for my schooling and give the rest to papa. I will not deny that even at that young age, I yearned for a path that will lead me somewhere, a place outside San Jacinto, and someday, be a man with some measure of attainment, a solid roof above my head, decent food on the table, the certainty of poverty being a thing of the past. A bidding from Don Rafael was filled with promise.

When the market square became visible, so did the human bustle. The vendors opened their stalls and people began haggling for prices. The tricycles were all lined up along the market's entrance. The *carenderias* teemed with drivers eating breakfast before they transported passengers to their destinations. I made my way through the crowd. That was the longest walk of my life, the walk away from home.

20

OMAR AND I NEVER TALKED about what happened that night. Perhaps I had been away too long for one of us to say something significant to each other. I myself do not recall giving the incident further thought. Perhaps it got buried as I moved from place to place and accrued new memories. After *Tio* Andres left last night, rain poured heavily as if rivaling the throb of my inner turmoil. I stepped outside in the rain, stood there in despair, lost, ambivalent. I believe I am a decent man; I have not harmed anyone. Yet, with all the years of decency, of righteousness, of following the rules, I have been a fool to believe that the world will reward me with a good life because I have earned it. Something was rending inside me.

Papa and Don Rafael were bound to meet even before they were born. One could say that their meeting was predestined if one views the world in that regard. Papa's father, *Lolo* Arturo was the head of the *sacadas* in one of the haciendas owned by the Madrigal family. As the head of the *sacadas*, the wages were entrusted to him, and he was responsible for distributing them to the rest of the sacadas. *Lolo* Arturo was also a skilled carpenter, and had a natural skill for nurturing plants. One day, Don Luisito, Don Rafael's father, asked *Lolo* Arturo to clear their garden from weeds and dead leaves and plant flower seeds. *Lolo* Arturo brought papa along with him.

It was nine-thirty in the morning when they arrived at the mansion. Papa was told to stay put, so he sat on a bench under the large acacia tree. His eyes surveyed the large estate. His head moved from right to left, left to right, and back again and again until he finally fixed his gaze at the two-storey mansion that glittered under the sunlight. He thought of their own small hut, its entire size was smaller than the Madrigals' living room. What else was on his young mind? He was enthralled by the house of the wealthy and he felt sorry for himself and his family. But the self-pity was short-lived, as it was then that his mind first opened to the world of possibilities, and it wandered long enough to ponder questions that none of his forefathers ever entertained. It was that moment of boredom, desire, and self-pity, all these combined, that led him to dream. Thoughts he had not accommodated before now occupied his mind. Education was the only way, he thought. He would have to go to school. He would have to beg his father and make a deal with his brother, Julio. No matter, his mind was set.

An hour passed and still no signs of *Lolo* Arturo, or of them leaving soon. Papa drew odd things and shapes on the damp soil using a stick. He thought he was alone there, free from prying eyes. He was not immediately aware that Don Rafael, then a boy about his age or slightly younger, had been watching him from the window of his room on the second floor. He had just woken up. He had a habit of lying in bed for another twenty minutes staring at his room's blue ceiling, after which he would go to the window and look at the view outside his room. He chiefly loved the way the sun shone across the land, the land that his family had owned for generations, all of which would be his one day. This was what his father told him last summer when they were having *merienda* in their front porch. His father's announcement did not surprise him. He knew early on that he was a privileged child. He had his own large playroom that housed all his toys. The way that he was attended to by the servants, the amount of national and international travelling he did, the schooling in Manila and unscheduled weekend visits to Sugbu, the regular summer holidays in Spain to see his *abuela*, he knew this was not the life of common people, certainly not the life of those who worked on their farm.

He got out of bed and walked towards the window. He was surprised to see papa. He hardly saw any child his age unless they were the children of his father's friends or colleagues. He knew from the boy's faded shirt, a size too small for him with patches of stains that he was from the hacienda. He knew, from the way the boy sat there wiping the sweat on his forehead with his arm, that he was one of the farm boys. These boys did not whine about their predicaments and inconveniences, they simply bowed their head in silence. He found that the poor had a generic way about them, a certain kind of slouch, the look of awe at the wealthy, and the boy sitting there, my father, embodied that stereotype. Rafael continued to observe the boy. He wanted to join him, have a chat, play, show him his toys; he was a kid after all. There was something that he felt deeply even at his young age, but he did not have yet a name for it—loneliness. Dinner conversations with his father were stiff and demanding. He was asked to speak in Spanish when discussing his school lessons and homework. He was expected to read one book every two weeks, and was asked to give an account of the story. It was only after much pleading on his part and his mother's intervention on his behalf that his father agreed to reduce the book reading to one every month. His father gave him drab lectures on history, civics, and current events, and quizzed Rafael to assess if he was paying attention to his discourse. Sometimes, when he and his father sat on the backseat of their gray Land Rover on their way to their mansion, he would see a group of farm kids playing and laughing, and a part of him wanted to step out of the vehicle and join them. He never had a constant playmate like other children. He did not even have a best friend.

He adjusted the jalousies to get a better view of what the boy was doing. Papa looked up at the second floor of the mansion and his eyes caught the figure of someone standing behind the window. He looked at the window and caught the stare of a boy. Papa stared back. He realized that the boy must be the son of the wealthy owner. Once or twice, someone had mentioned the rich man's son, a young boy who quietly observed his surroundings as though he was gathering and storing all sorts of information in his head. No one knew what this boy thought or felt.

And so their eyes met. Their eyes met, and their fate was sealed. Of course, there was a vast divide, one boy on the fortress looking down at the world below him, and the other one with bowed head, submitting to the verity of his lowly life. Papa withdrew his gaze as though he was embarrassed, apologetic for looking at the boy, Rafael, in the eye. Instead he looked down at the ground and resumed playing with the stick he was holding. But Rafael continued to look at him. He and the boy would meet again, Rafael thought.

PART TWO

"HELLO? BENJAMIN! BENJAMIN! Are you there? Are you awake?"

"I am here, *tio*. The door is open. You can come in."

"Good morning, Benjamin. Jesus! It's dark in here! I'll draw the curtains and let a bit of light in! My God, you drank all these by yourself? Did you ever get any sleep last night?"

"Not much. I had a dream that reminded me of papa. Then I woke up and had a hard time going back to sleep. What's the latest news about Don Rafael, *tio*? Is he in town yet? Is he dead or alive?"

"No news yet, Benjamin, but tomorrow we shall find out for sure. Ramon is in the city now but will arrive here tomorrow. In any event, Ramon will know Don Rafael's plight, dead or alive, and will immediately let me know. I trust him."

"I hope the bastard is alive, *Tio* Andres. I want to get it over and done with. I have thought it through numerous times and I have made up my mind about it."

"About what? With your state of mind right now, it is best to give yourself time before rushing to make a big decision. What are you planning to do anyway?

"I am not going to tell you what I plan to do. It is best if no one knows anything, especially you, *tio*. That way, you will not be implicated. I have to protect you."

"Protect me from what? I have lived a hard life, and nothing scares me anymore. I am the only family you have left. Whatever you do, people will never believe that I know nothing especially after this tragedy. And who will listen to me if I plead ignorance? I am nobody. But I do not care about that. If I die, I die. If it is my time, nothing in this world can prevent that from happening. Benjamin, listen to me. You are like a son to me. If I am right in thinking that you are planning something you may regret, I advise you against being rash. And besides…"

He was about to say something but paused. I knew what he was going to say; he was going to remind me about God and sin and redemption. To which I would reply, to hell with God and his rewards in heaven.

"Besides what, *tio*? You yourself said he's the worst kind of human being. The worst piece of scum. If I seek revenge, doesn't he deserve it? I am sure I speak for the majority who suffer in silence because of fear, because they have no choice. You know this is true. When I was a boy, I heard stories from you and your friends about his depravity. You yourself once witnessed how a farm worker died from a gunshot because he was forced to participate in the Russian roulette that Don Rafael loved to play when he was drunk. Should I even mention the despicable low wages he pays compared to other landowners, and all because he owns the lands that the families live on, and he knows they have nowhere else to go?

"Yes, you are right about that. He is no saint."

"I have had time to contemplate, *tio*, and I have been blind. But it is all clear to me now. All those hushed talks when I was a boy living in his house about his abuses are true. I've been a witness to his temper when he thought no one was around to hear him. I can only imagine what he actually did when he was displeased, how cruel and abusive he must have been. But I looked the other way, choosing to see instead, how kind and generous he was to me. But you know very well what kind of man he is, *tio*. Now you cannot tell me that he does not deserve to suffer. Just this once, set aside God and his teachings. Think about the people in this town, our people. Think about papa, and Omar. Don't their lives matter too?

"Benjamin, please listen to me. I know you are angry and you have every right to feel that way. And what you just said is all true. But now is not the time to talk about it or dwell on it. You must pull yourself together, Benjamin. There is something more important and urgent that you need to attend to right this moment."

"What could be more important than this?"

He heads to the door and tells me to follow him outside. A young boy is standing several feet away from the door and *Tio* Andres motions him to approach us.

"This is Alonso, your nephew, Omar's son."

"Omar's son?"

"Are you my *Tio* Benjamin?" the boy asks with wide eyes.

"Hello, Alonso. Yes, I am your *Tio* Benjamin," I say, staring at him in disbelief.

He runs to me and leaps into my arms with full abandon. I carry and hold him tight, my charming, orphan boy. Then he releases himself from me and says he wants to go by the mango tree. I want him to stay but I do not hold him back. "Okay, do not go too far." It is as if I see Omar all over again, as he runs off and disappears from our sight.

Tio Andres scratches his head. "I am as shocked as you. I cannot believe it. All this happened just around five o'clock this morning. Juan, his grandfather knocked on my door and came with the boy. They live in Silaw, about nine hours away from here. He has been the one taking care of the child. But now he is ill and could no longer take care of him. His wife passed away four years ago. Juan's daughter, Rosario, Alonso's mother, did not tell Omar that she was carrying his child. Their love affair was a secret from the very start. She had promised to marry a policeman from their town. She thought that marrying him would ease her life, but she did not love the man. She fled town when she got pregnant. When the boy turned two, Rosario showed up at Silaw to leave the boy in the care of Juan. She then went back to the city, apparently worked as a dancer in one of the rowdy nightclubs there. Got hooked on drugs and into all sorts of trouble. Then she went to work in Japan, and Juan has never heard from her since then. He went to her last known address in the city and met with a friend of hers, but the friend said that there are rumors that she got involved with the wrong crowd, but no one has heard from her. To make matters worse, the friend's acquaintance said that she heard from another person who came back from Japan that Rosario was involved in a fatal accident, but no one knows what became of her after that. Rosario revealed to Juan during her pregnancy that Omar is the father, told him that Omar lives in San Jacinto, but she begged him not to tell anyone, that she would be the one to tell Omar when the right time came. Alas it never happened."

"He knows that Omar has a brother, even knows that the brother lives in the States. He heard about Omar's death from a relative of his named Pedro who resides in *barangay* Kawit, and it was that same relative who suggested to Juan to come talk to me first before approaching you. Apparently, Pedro and I met once or twice at some fiesta somewhere. I meet so many people at fiestas that I do not remember Pedro, but I will recognize his face when I see him. It was Pedro who told him about Omar's death. Juan figured that the brother, you, should be coming home for his funeral, so he decided to come here right away. He said he was too ashamed to present the boy to you personally because to ask you this is such a huge undertaking. If not for his ill health, he wouldn't have come here. He dropped hints that he's not going to get better. He looked very pale and coughed a lot. He sends his apologies as well as his gratitude. What he told the boy was that he will be staying with his *tio* for a while. He left in time to catch the next bus home. He left in tears."

"The boy knows that his father is dead. But not from this tragedy. I mean, he was told from the beginning that Omar got into a motorcycle accident and died. It is very eerie to me, almost seemed like a premonition. For the mother to have told the child his father is dead, removes from us this painful task of telling him that Omar is now dead, as he grew up believing that he had already died. Poor child. Of course, it is much more complicated than this, but maybe we should not worry about the complications right now. Maybe it is best to deal with things as they come. Alonso only has you, Benjamin. You are the best person to raise him. Juan believes that the mother will not come back for him. It is very sad. The child, what a spitting image of Omar."

"*Tio* Andres, this is too much for me to comprehend right now. I don't know what to say. I look at him and I see Omar when he was a boy. I am in utter shock. If you don't mind, I just need a moment here."

"Of course, son. Take your time. I will watch over Alonso."

I go inside the house and head upstairs, as though there is something up there that I need to check. I am shaking; I do not think I can make it upstairs. I think I will stop here and sit on the stairs for a while. I must find something to give to Alonso while I gather my thoughts. Perhaps I should give the coloring books and crayons that Cora asked me to send to his nephew. Maybe some pens and paper to draw and write on. Maybe nothing, I do not know. Should I call Cora and tell her that I have a nephew, ask her what to do, what to say? I have a nephew playing outside, his young life already marked with great losses and what I want to do is go to the kitchen and reach for a bottle of alcohol. How do I raise this child? What do I tell him about this world? A sudden cold wind brushes through my skin and I feel as though Omar just breezed through me. I look up as if to catch the words he is whispering, pressing, echoing through the walls. I go to my room and stand before his ashes. *Omar, I know I have caused you pain and disappointment, but you have to forgive me because you have a son left in my care, and I need your help. I am scared, I do not know what to do. I do not want to fail him. He is a wonderful boy, Omar, just like you were. And he will grow up knowing your goodness, that I promise you. Watch over us, my dear brother.*

I decide to go back downstairs and face them, and as I walk it feels as though I am staggering through a house I do not own, knocking into furniture, hitting walls, unable to find my way. I am walking into the unknown. I am walking into vagueness. *Tio* Andres has not moved from where I left him. He is smoking, pensive, looking at Alonso who seems to have found something to occupy him. We are both quiet now. We are simply looking at the child as though we have not seen a child before, as though we are both thinking, *What now? What happens now?*

"Do you want to be alone right now, Benjamin? I know this is overwhelming, to say the least. I can take the child home with me. Your *tia* and I will look after him until we figure something out. You can take all the time you want. You just tell me when you want us to come back. If you prefer that we stay, then we shall stay."

I do not know if I want to be alone or should be left alone. It seems that all I am capable of doing at the moment is stand still until I get tired, until my nephew comes happily running to me.

"I would like both of you to stay, *tio*. I know you rose at dawn but if you want to go home and take a rest, please do so. Alonso can stay here. I can manage. I will take care of my nephew."

"Okay. I will do that and take care of a few things at home. Perhaps it is good that you spend time alone with him, get acquainted, feel comfortable."

I feel a tremendous affection for *Tio* Andres right now. "*Tio*, I do not know how I can ever repay you and *tia*. Both of you have always been there for us. We have put you through a lot, but not once have I heard you complain or express regret or change your attitude towards us. You were always there for papa and Omar, especially when I was not around. And now you are here for me and Alonso."

"Benjamin, we are family, and that is what we do for each other. This is what life is about, to take care of one another whatever the circumstances may be. When I leave here, I trust that you will not do anything rash and foolish. Can you promise me this? Please. At least do it for your nephew."

"I promise, *tio*."

"A child is always a blessing. You may not see it that way now. As soon as I hear any news about Don Rafael, I shall come see you right away and we can discuss whatever plans you have in mind. He will have his day of reckoning and it will come to pass when he least expects it. I haven't mentioned to you that the farm workers, all of us from all the haciendas in San Jacinto, are going to form a union. We are going to go on strike. We are in the early stages of the plan, but we are going to take action. We've had enough. It's about time we speak up otherwise our lives and the generations to come will never improve. I will keep you informed of any development. Well, I will see you later. If you need anything, anything at all, you know you can come knock on our door anytime. God bless you, son."

He turns around and walks toward Alonso who is running in his direction. It is another moment of parting for the child. *Tio* Andres fixes his hair and tells him something I cannot make out. The child nods and they both embrace. Alonso stands still, his gaze fixed at *Tio* Andres as he goes on his way until he is out of sight. I cannot help but wonder what he is thinking. Does he want to go back to his grandfather? Does he miss him already? Is he sad? I recall Omar standing by the door watching papa leave for work, all of his emotions contained in that vacant, distant gaze, revealing nothing and everything. I then thought that perhaps the sight of papa leaving home each morning drew up in him a fear that he might not come back.

"*Tio*? *Tio*?"

"Yes. I am sorry, Alonso. I got lost in my thoughts."

"You kept looking over there, you didn't notice me standing next to you. What were you thinking, *tio*?"

"Many things. Random things. Adults overthink sometimes."

"Like what things?"

"Like what time it is, how hungry you are. Or how tired."

We stand next to each other witnessing the world pass us by. The sun is waiting to burst, but not quite yet, not until the stubborn clouds disassemble. I put my right arm around his bony shoulders. I feel the world rumble below my feet. Soon trucks filled with farm workers will inhabit the road, men and women will carry on with their usual tasks. I wonder what else this day will reveal.

"I'm thirsty, *tio*."

"Come, let's go to the kitchen and have breakfast."

We eat the food that *Tio* Andres brought this morning. He tells me that his grandfather is ill, that he is a fisherman, and that he tagged along with him wherever he went. He is not afraid of the water. "I am a good swimmer", he announces with pride. He carries on with more personal details: he is seven years old, his birthday is August 25th; he loves *pansit* and fried *danggit*; after dinner, he and his *Lolo* Juan listen to the radio where he would eventually fall asleep beside him. "Did you see a rainbow this morning?" he inquires. His friend, Toto, is afraid of spiders but he, on the other hand, does not fear them. He lets them crawl on his palms and arms then lets them lose on the soil. Treasure this moment now, this innocence, the way he is sitting up straight and eating the food on his plate with gusto, I say to myself. Remember his stories, remember all of it, every word if possible, every pause, the pitch, the child-like wonder, because before you know it, all this will pass quickly and never come again. Remember this day, this room, even the eddy of light now piercing through the windows, the after-smell of last night's rain, hold it all dearly before he becomes bruised by his family's secrets. He does not mention his mother. I should ask *Tio* Andres what he knows of her. His fingernails need cleaning, his hair needs a trim. Did he bring clothes with him? Shoes? He and I need to go shopping for essential supplies. I make a list in my head.

Omar was his son's age when I left home to live at Don Rafael's house. I visited my family on weekends. I indulged Omar, did anything he wanted us to do to make up for my absence. When time came for me to leave again, he sulked in the corner. "Don't go yet, don't go," he begged. And I left home carrying the weight of those words in my heart. But as time passed, I learned to do what needed to be done every Sunday— to put the knapsack on my shoulder and say goodbye. No words could have appeased Omar, not even the promise of my return.

Alonso proceeds to tell me that he slept the entire time on the bus coming to San Rafael. He asks about the hut.

"Does anyone live there?"

"No one now. We used to live there, your papa and I and your *Lolo* Pablo."

"Can I take a look inside, *Tio*?"

I am not ready to take him there. I fear the questions that he may ask. I fear my own instability. I prefer that he and I go to the sea and fly kites on the beach. Or do something practical, like buy groceries or clothes for him. But I cannot refuse the child. I wish to indulge him; that is the least I can do. I put more rice and adobo on his plate and he welcomes the second serving. Clearly he is hungry and seems comfortable in his new surroundings. Does he realize that his grandfather entrusted him to me? I doubt he grasps this. And if he does, he does not exhibit concern or confusion or sadness. A hundred things occupy my mind but for now, I focus on this moment, he and I partaking on food, chatting, having some sense of normalcy. I recall the feeling of being full, as he is now, and how it was at times, in my youth, the best feeling in the world.

"Yes, you can take a look. Did you bring clothes with you?"

"Yes, it's in the plastic bag outside. And my toy car is in there too. A jeep."

I know what that toy jeep looks like. I had one of those when I was a kid. It is made of plastic, and sold by the vendors in the town square. It was a delight for me when, after the boredom I felt during Mass, papa would surprise us with the announcement that Omar and I could each buy a toy. We picked the plastic cars because they were the cheapest. I understand why my nephew did not forget to bring the toy jeep with him. It is possibly his favorite toy, and I am certain that he does not have many.

"I think it's a good day to go to the beach. The sun is now up. I doubt that it will rain. We could have a picnic, build sandcastles, and you can even go for a swim if you'd like. We could have a lot of fun. What do you think?"

I do not care much about going to the beach but I am more inclined to sit on the sand and drink beer than go to the hut. I want him to have a pleasant distraction and not witness me mull over my life, and his, and ours together.

"I would like that, *Tio*. What do we do first? Go to the hut or the beach?"

We decide to toss a coin, heads for the hut and tails for the beach.

"Well, off to the hut first then. Are you finished eating?"

"Yes, I'm so full."

"I'm going to put the dishes away and then I have to do a few things. Why don't you go check your bag of clothes?"

"Okay, *Tio*. I'll play outside."

I take the dishes to the sink and look out the window. The sky that was cheerless is now an Eden of light blue. The backyard has two mango trees and two guava trees. Plants thrive. The white roses look poignant in their innocence. The weeds, shrubs and flowers co-exist amicably. Peace falls there, day and night, no matter what the season is. A yellow butterfly joins in, now a bird (maya?) hovers above the crown and decides to rest on a branch. How wonderful to catch the world filled with such serenity.

I open a bottle of San Miguel and sit on the chair, looking at how well-kept the kitchen is, how organized, how unlived. I have not had a moment to enjoy the house. The construction was fully finished about eight months ago. I felt such elation when I first received the news. My co-workers noticed my general joviality. "You seem unusually happy today." "Someone's in a good mood," they remarked. Am I that morose, unable to even feign enthusiasm that a slight change in my disposition was so obvious to elicit a reaction? They said they caught me humming tunes as I walked the hallways, greeting everyone, patients and staff alike, with a new kind of smile. They speculated. Some thought I had started getting laid every night. Others thought I got a huge raise or bonus. One even thought that one of the patients who was fond of me made me a beneficiary in her will. I let them carry on with their speculations. Only Cora knew the reason. That evening when I received the photos of the house from the contractor, Cora came to my apartment and brought a bottle of champagne to celebrate. It was my first time drinking champagne. It took me back to the days of living at Don Rafael's house, as there was an abundance of champagne and wine when they had guests, and I thought then that that must be what the wealthy people drank. When Cora and I had made a toast, I felt great pride thinking that I had made it in life. The house, the champagne, I thought they were representations of an accomplished life. Cora stayed over that night. When I was certain that she was asleep, I got out of bed and went to the balcony. I opened a can of beer and made a toast to papa and Omar. I felt their absence intensely that evening. Papa did not live to see the house finished. I intended for him to live somewhere comfortable for the remainder of his life but alas it was not to be. I went to bed refusing to succumb to the sadness thinking of them, and having Cora's company that night helped me redeem the pride I felt about owning a house.

Cora comes to my mind. I want to frame her drawings and put them on the walls. I want her creativity to fill the corners of the house. I have yet to tell her about my plight. It was two years ago when internet, cable, and mobile services became available in San Jacinto. I had planned on driving up south and deliver the package that Cora sent for her nephew, Carlos. He is the ten-year old son of her closest sister, Carmencita, or Cita, as she is called. When Cora ran away from home, it was Cita that she most worried about as she was the youngest and was always frail, prone to illnesses, and often unattended. So here is Cora making up for lost time and for whatever happened to Cita in the past (some unspecified trauma of sorts) by sending her money and goods every month, toys for her son, and whatever else she needed to sustain the daily living of her household that includes a drunk and lazy husband, and apparently, a demanding mother-in-law. With Cora's financial support, Cita managed to get a teaching degree. Her pay as a public school teacher is not enough, not with a perpetually jobless husband who demands certain comforts. There is the brand-new motorcycle and a flat screen television that she pays for every month; the air conditioner turned on every night when he goes to sleep, but not for the relief of the cold air but for the sound the air conditioner makes that strangely soothes him and gives him a restful sleep. Cora tolerates these unreasonable demands on her money. She couldn't say no to her sister once she started sobbing on the phone and spoke of the suffering she otherwise quietly endured every day. Cora once advised Cita to leave her husband. It can be done, it has been done by many, and Cora would naturally support her, but no, Cita is too Catholic to even entertain such a notion. "Am I not bound to my husband until death do us part? I made a vow and I intend to keep it. Besides, what will people say?" "But my son needs a father." All this would cause her even more distress, Cita claimed. Cora never brought it up again. She even felt guilty suggesting an annulment. It was no wonder that not much explanation was needed for Cora to understand my protectiveness towards Omar, as she felt the same way towards Cita.

This is the first time that I am looking at the layout of the kitchen. I am not one to care for details of color or kind of material, the subtlety or extravagance of style, but at this moment the pride of being a homeowner is slowly making its way back to me. The dining table is made of teak. The chairs are comfortable. The kitchen walls are white, the shelves and drawers are light green. The windows are big enough, and well situated to allow sufficient light to come in. It is equipped with everything essential that a cook may need to prepare a fancy meal. The plates, saucers, bowls, and cutlery are more than enough for a family of five. I had planned on having a house blessing and a big party (I thought of inviting Cora). I had imagined the scenario would take place in this very kitchen; all three of us, neighbors and friends, cooking food, eating and drinking together. Our cheerful voices would waft throughout the room, with our happy stories. The imagery in my head is the opposite of this moment, bereft of laughter and abundant with silence. I suppose I should be glad I have this house. And now, suddenly, a nephew.

And here he comes bringing the plastic bag of clothes with him. "Found it right where I said I put it," he says, and puts the bag on one of the chairs. He smells of morning heat, much like any child in San Jacinto who has stayed out too long in the sun. He takes out his toy jeep and lets it run on the kitchen table.

"Do you want some beer?" I ask seriously though of course I am joking.

"Not now. When I'm older, I'm sure I'll have some of that and we can drink together," he says with equal seriousness and we both laugh.

I was once a boy his age and I can tell he is beginning to get bored. I am thinking of food again, what to feed him for lunch. I have not forgotten my promise to take him to the hut, as I know that he has not forgotten it either. I finish my beer and keep my word.

"In the beginning, there was only the sky and the sea, and between them was a hawk. One day the hawk roused the sea until it burst its waters against the sky. The sky reacted by creating many islands so the sea could no longer rise. Then the sky told the hawk to build her nest on the islands and leave the sky and the sea alone. The hawk was now glad that there was land.

At this time, the marriage of the land breeze and the sea breeze took place. They had a child—a bamboo. One day, the bamboo struck the feet of the hawk. This made the hawk mad and she pecked the bamboo until it slit open in two. From one section there emerged a man, and from the other, a woman.

Then the earthquake asked what should be done with the man and the woman. The birds and the fishes said that they should marry, and so it was done. The couple bore many children.

After some time, the parents grew tired of their idle and restless children and thought of a place they could send them to. More time passed, and the children grew in number and the parents became very weary at the lack of peace. Desperate and anxious, the father got hold of a stick and began beating the children.

The children got scared and dashed off in different directions. Some hid behind the walls, and some sought shelter inside the rooms. Some ran to the fireplace, others ran outside. And there are those who fled to the sea.

Now it turned out that those who went into the hidden rooms became the chiefs of the islands, and those who hid behind the walls became slaves. Those who ran outside became free men, and those who hid in the fireplace became dark skinned people. Those who went to the sea were absent for a very long time. And when they came back, they became the white people."

"Bamboo? Why a bamboo, *Tio* Benjamin?"

"It's a Filipino myth. When I was your age, that's exactly what I asked your *Lolo* Pablo. Myths are part of our tradition, our culture. The story has been handed down to us for many generations. There is another thing about bamboos that I will tell you."

"Tell me."

"Your papa Omar has been growing bamboo plants in the backyard. A bamboo rarely flowers, and when it does, all the bamboo plants in the world flower too.

"The world? Even America where you live?

"Yes, even America. Do you want to take care of your papa Omar's bamboos?"

"Yes, I want to take care of them. They're going to have flowers. You'll see, *tio*."

"You know, Alonso, that when it flowers, it means good luck."

"Really? They will flower, *tio*. Then we'll have good luck. You'll see."

We are both sitting on the wooden bench in the garden. When mama passed away, the three of us did our best to keep the garden alive. It was our small gesture of honor to her. We kept growing all sorts of plants to keep it flourishing.

"Your grandmother started this garden. She passed away when your papa was a baby. We all took turns taking care of it."

"I'll watch over the garden too, *tio*. I'll water the plants. Maybe I'll find some spiders."

I take his hand and together we walk towards the hut. I hide my anxiety with frivolous talk.

"We should go to the town square later and get you more clothes and a pair of shoes. And toys. Any toy you want. Do you play with marbles? Your papa and I had quite a collection. We had jars full of them. This here was our playground extending all the way over there where the hacienda ends. You can't even see the end from here. That's how big our playground was, and that's how far we walked. We flew kites. Tomorrow we shall make our own kite. Have you ever chewed sugarcane? We used to do that and though there is nothing extraordinary about it, the taste is like no other. So pure. And this hut was where your great-grandparents lived. It used to be just a simple one without the veranda and the extension in the back. Over time, the floors were changed, and the roof, and whatever else that needed to be fixed. Well, I suppose you better go in now. I'll wait for you out here and enjoy the sun. Have I told you that I only arrived here yesterday, and I didn't get to enjoy the sun much? In America, there are four seasons so there are months you don't get to enjoy warmth like this. What a beautiful day this is, don't you think? Oh, remind me to unpack my luggage. I have a toy to give you. Well, you best go in now. I'll be out here."

Off he goes. I try to shift my attention somewhere else while fear coiled staunchly in my head. Someone is calling my name. I turn towards the street and I see *Tia* Gloria walking towards me.

"Benjamin! I was on my way to your house but I saw you here."

"*Tia*! I'm sorry I haven't had the chance to see you. I am so glad you are here."

Tears fall from her eyes when we embrace. How comforting it is to be in her arms.

"Thank you for the *pasalubong*. Those imported chocolates are heavenly. They won't last long with my sweet tooth. I brought you food. I know food is the last thing on your mind right now, but you have got to eat."

"Thank you, *tia*. Actually, I was just thinking of food. I am sure you know about Alonso."

"Yes, yes, I do. Poor child. I brought food for both of you. I am worried about you, son. Talk to me. Tell me what's on your mind. You do not have to feel alone in all of this. Your *tio* and I are here for you. You know that."

"I know, *tia*. By the way, thank you for looking after the house. Only in your hands would the house be so clean and well-kept like that."

"I am happy to do it for you. It doesn't require work anyway. There is no mess to be cleaned. Besides, it's good to walk there after dinner, stretch a bit and get some air. It gives your *tio* and me a short break from each other. Forty-four years of marriage. Even twenty minutes being apart from each other is divine. Where is Alonso?"

"He's inside the hut. He wanted to take a look. Maybe he got curious. I got emotional when I went there yesterday. Not ready to go inside again if I can help it. That's why I am standing out here."

"You have so much on your shoulders right now. Frankly I don't know how you are coping, especially after all that revelation about your papa and Omar, and now about your nephew. You found the truth, but it is a very harsh one, and I don't know if that will ever give you peace. It wasn't easy for your *tio* to tell you. It weighed on him for days. He thought of telling you that he drowned by accident, but with the cremation, he thought you might be suspicious. He said that he will do what he feels is the right thing and the right thing was to tell you the truth about everything."

She lifts her left hand and uses it to wipe her tears. She takes quick glances at the hut while she speaks. Perhaps she wants to know the moment Alonso comes out of the door. Perhaps she does not want him to see her crying.

"Don't tell your *tio* this, but last night, he cried and couldn't go to sleep. He felt unsettled. He was unsure if he did the right thing telling you the truth. He was sorry for the pain it caused you, and worried too about what that pain might compel you to do."

"*Tia*, he was right to tell me the truth. Don Rafael does not deserve my respect. Yes, I have been blind. After all, he has shown me nothing but kindness. But that was all a charade. A man who shows goodness on one front and does evil on the

other is a deceiver. I am filled with guilt and regret. I feel I am
to blame for everything. It was all due to my childish dreams."

"No, I am not going to let you carry on with that foolish talk.
It is never wrong to dream, Benjamin. We all have one but not
everyone is brave enough to pursue it. Your papa had the exact
dreams for you as you had for yourself. He was very proud of you.
He was happy about what you had become, an accomplished and
responsible man. Above all, he was happy to see you live the life
you've always wanted. Perhaps you regret moving away, thinking
that had you stayed, this wouldn't have happened. Perhaps you
are thinking that all his sacrifice led to tragedy. Perhaps. But then
here you are, you accomplished your dreams. You are satisfied
with your lot, are you not? So, all is not in vain. You were not
meant to live here, Benjamin. Not in those years anyway. If you
did, you would have lived an unfulfilled life. Even as a child, we
knew you were destined for great things. We all make sacrifices.
In this case, it was your father who chose to make that sacrifice, as
fathers and mothers do. Now you have a nephew who needs you.
Perhaps this is your other purpose in life. I know it doesn't make
sense in the way that, say, science makes sense, or mathematics.
Perhaps one will never know why life is this way or that way."

"Did he regret doing it?"

"No. He longed for you and Omar to have a better life, one
he never had. That was most important to him."

"I mean, did he regret killing someone?"

"I don't know. I cannot speak for him. We all pay for the
choices we make. It was a consequence he did not foresee.
We may be poor, but we are decent people. We do not inflict
harm on anyone let alone commit murder. He simply trusted
that monster, trusted that his offer was sincere. It wasn't free
of course, but he never thought it would cost him that. He

didn't have a choice in that moment. Well, you know the story. I understand your regrets. One day, son, you're going to have to learn to forgive yourself."

Alonso steps out of the hut and walks towards us. *Tia* Gloria hurriedly wipes the tears from her eyes.

"*Lola* Gloria!" he shouts with glee. He runs to her and hugs her as though they have not seen each other in a long time though they have met only briefly, when he arrived at *tio* and *tia*'s doorstep at dawn.

"How are you, my dear? Are you hungry? I have some *turon*."

"I love *turon*."

"I know you do so I made sure to bring you some."

Tia Gloria hands him a piece. The three of us form a circle. The sun shines upon us.

"I saw photos of my papa. He looked exactly like he was in my dream. Handsome and strong."

"You've dreamt of your papa?"

"Yes. We were walking along the shore, much like the shore near *Lolo* Juan's house. We held hands and walked as far as the shore led us. We didn't get tired. We laughed a lot." He asks for another piece of *turon*.

"Perhaps we should walk back to the house and eat there, and have some refreshments."

"Alas, I cannot join you both right this minute. But I shall bring dinner for you later. My dear child, do you have any food requests?"

"Umm, I don't know. I'll eat whatever food you bring, *lola*."

"Very well, then. Get ready to be fed. All right, I'll see you both later. Bye for now."

I embrace her, and whisper thank you. When she is at a distance from us, Alonso and I start walking.

"You know, we used to spend some nights at their house when we were young. Their children, our cousins, were our playmates. *Tia* is a fantastic cook. Her food is delicious. You doing okay?"

"I'm fine, *tio.*"

Inside the house, we sit in the living room. I tell him that this is his home. I show him the rooms in the house. I show him his room. He sits on the bed and remarks how soft it is. I am tired. I am very tired. I want to go to bed. I want to sleep. I want to hug him. I want peace. I want to take away all his sadness.

"There's something I wish to tell you. I'm afraid it's a serious matter but it is important that you know."

"Okay, *tio*. Please tell me what it is."

"Sometimes, when people die, they want to be buried in the ground."

"Yes, like my *Lola* Truding. She was *Lolo* Juan's wife."

"Yes, like your *Lola* Truding. Sometimes, other people want to be cremated. And when they are cremated, their body turns into ashes. And the ashes are kept by their loved ones. Your papa wanted to be cremated. His ashes are in a jar in my room. Now, this is a big responsibility on your part. I want you to take care of his ashes only because you are the person that he loved the most. You can put it in your room or some other place that you like. If you don't want to move it for now, that is fine also. If there ever comes a time that you want to spread his ashes somewhere as some people do, any place that you think would make him happy, and that you like, you can also do that. I know this is a lot to comprehend right now. You can ask me questions anytime. You can choose not to do anything right now. Or you can choose not to do anything at all. It's okay, but I feel compelled to tell you all this because it is important that you know your father is right here in this house with you. And it is quite an honor to be chosen to be the keeper of a loved one's ashes. It is overwhelming and a big task but that's what we do for our loved ones."

"I understand, *tio*. I think I know what responsibility means. It's like me taking care of the bamboo plant and *lola's* garden. Or *Lolo* Juan taking care of me. Or you taking care of me. I also know that my papa loves me. In my dream he told me that. He is always around. When I lived in *Lolo* Juan's house, I felt his presence. Especially when I'm in the sea. It's like he and I know each other already. I want to see papa's ashes, *tio*. May I see it right now?"

I make myself a drink in the kitchen and take my nephew upstairs to see his father. That was the most difficult conversation in my life, but Alonso made it easy for me.

Maybe there is a God after all. Maybe God doesn't live in heaven. Maybe it is your loved one laughing in your dreams. Maybe it is grace arriving at your door unannounced, dressed in dirty shirt and shorts, with small hands clasped together as if in prayer. It could be your mother's soft hands touching your cheek or the depth of your father's quiet love. Perhaps you don't have to spend your entire life questioning its existence or look far, because it is always around you, present, right at this moment.

I am exhausted. I could fall into bed and sleep for days. What is that circle of glaring light? It is all quiet now. I can hear the sky and land converse in a secret language. I am moved by this stillness.

I DON'T KNOW WHAT WOKE ME UP. Alonso is not here. I go check his room, but he is not there. I panic at the thought that he left the house and went back to his grandfather. I search the room for something that he might have left behind, but there is nothing. The room looks like it was untouched or unoccupied. I sit on the bed for a while. Tomorrow is a very important day. Tomorrow I will find out if Don Rafael is alive or not. Tomorrow, I will honor life by taking another. Tomorrow, I may lose everything—my name, my possessions, my dreams, my entire life. But first, I must check on my nephew and make sure he is all right. Why does it seem as though I am the one who needs him more than he needs me? I contemplate what will become of him when I am gone. My heart weakens at the thought of him being alone, how he will survive, how he will ever be able to live a decent life. Already, I am thinking about what to say to him; my parting words. Farewell, my child, and fare well in the world out there; these words were once said to me by papa. In my head I compose a letter to him. *My dear Alonso, I woke up to the sun's radiance filling my room and for a moment, I was taken back to my childhood mornings when the same northern sky spoke of the gladness of another day spent thinking of what your papa and I could do to amuse ourselves outdoors. We never ran out of things to do, and even in our boredom, we managed to do something fun together. And witnessing the glow in my room when I woke up, what also came to mind was the concept of light, whether literal or symbolic. Forgive this note. It has to do with light and life and my own nostalgia. I search for words that will make a difference, but I realize that I do not have all the answers, so I will tell you now that there will be many occasions throughout your life when you won't immediately understand situations, people, even yourself, because life is a continuous unfolding. Sometimes when I am feeling a bit down, I take a solitary walk, and my heart leaps at the sight of flowers, or the sound of waves crashing, or the way the sunlight hits the roof of old houses. Always find time for quietude;*

find time to experience nature. It will teach you and speak to you in ways that nothing else can. All you have to do is be present and pay attention.

When I talk about light, I speak of things that sustain you and remind you of the good in this world. It could be a memory of something, like the sound of a loved one's laughter or an act of kindness, or the words Thank you and I'm sorry.

I want us to be comforted by honesty, so let me tell you that with light comes darkness. Life can be hard, people can be cruel to you even though you have done nothing to deserve it. You will live among the lost, the oppressed, the privileged, the corrupt, the darkest of souls. But always, how you react will make the difference. There is a force out there much bigger than ourselves. When I talk about light, I speak about all the wonderment, simple or grand, that makes you smile and laugh and dream and aspire. Alonso, find your light and you won't be lost; you'll come through even though you have lost sight of everyone you hold dear. Be brave. When I talk about light, I speak about you, and here I stop because there are no words sufficient enough to catch this meaning. Take care of yourself.

I feel like an utter failure composing this farewell note in my head. Perhaps I should write a will instead, and bequeath everything I own to him.

Wind wafts through the open window. I have the urge to feel it against my face so I stand up and peek my head outside. And there he is, my dear Alonso playing in the garden. A butterfly is hovering above him. And Alonso is amused by this. He moves left and right, forward and backward, trying to see if the butterfly follows him. Then he stands still, and waits for the butterfly to come closer to him. And I am astounded at what I am seeing, the butterfly lands on his right shoulder and stays there. He laughs with a laughter that can only belong to the innocence of a child. And all I hear now is the music of his laughter, and what emerges from all this, from looking at him so alive, so trusting, so full of grace, the leaves dancing with the wind, the sun benevolent with light, what emerges are tears from my eyes. And I am crying, crying like I have never cried before. Crying for the past, present, and future, for all that was betrayed and broken, for a life of despair and hope and the unknown. And it seems like it is in my dream, my cry turning into a bellow so strong and loud and clamorous as though the fury that has been lurking in the depths is finally being released.

PART THREE

"IT WAS MANY YEARS AGO when he called me and said he wanted to execute these documents and name you as beneficiary of his estate. I did not know who you were or what his relation was to you. I asked him if he was sure about it, and he said yes. I asked him three times and he confirmed without any hesitation. He phoned me about five months ago. He said he'll be away on a long trip and should anything happen to him, he wanted to make sure that his testamentary documents were in order, and that all his wishes were to be carried out exactly as he intended. Maybe he had a premonition about his death. So, young man, is this really what you want to do with the land? The Agrarian Reform Law allows you to still keep a sizeable portion of it before the government takes away the rest to be distributed to the small farmers."

"Yes, I am sure, Attorney Vere. I want to donate all of it."

"All of it? You are not going to keep a little for yourself, a hectare, half a hectare, one fourth? For the future, perhaps?"

"No, sir."

"Once you make your final decision, there is no undoing it."

"I understand. My decision stands."

"As you wish then. The *sacadas* will be happy to be free from being held, enslaved I dare say, by the big landowners. Don Rafael must have trusted you to know what to do with the land."

"I don't know about that. Only he knows what his intentions were when he named me beneficiary of his estate."

"Oh, believe me, son. There can only be trust and love for you. He could have named his relatives as beneficiaries, could have donated it to charities, but he chose you instead. That you are the recipient of his generosity is a rare thing because you are not of his blood. What a heart of gold that man had. May God bless his soul. Anyway, as to the matter of Alonso's adoption, I will prepare the documents. You let me know when you want this filed.

"I will. Thank you."

"Anything else I can do for you, Benjamin?"

"No, sir, that is all."

Benjamin shakes Mr. Vere's hand then leaves the office. Grief has made it difficult for him to talk to and be around others, and it was out of necessity that he had to drive to the city to finalize the documents. He feels tremendous relief as he walks away from the attorney's office.

It is an ordinary afternoon in Sugbu. Benjamin steps outside and inhales the fumes of the increasingly booming city. He is shocked at the long queue of cars; traffic of this sort was unheard of before. A sentimental man, he decides to walk farther down the road to reach his old university. He has not been back there since he graduated. He used to walk this street every day after his last class was over. He searches for the old stores he passed by on his way to the junction of Sepulveda and Santol, streets where he waited for the *jeepney* to take him home. He remembers a *sari-sari* store where he bought a bottle of cold Royal Tru-Orange whenever he got thirsty. He recalls, too, a small photo shop owned by a man named Simeon, where all the students went to have their photographs taken and developed. Those stores are gone now, replaced by a bank and a McDonald's. He feels a certain sense of loss though those places were inconsequential to him. What he remembers most of all was himself as a student years ago clad in jeans and shirt, carrying a notebook and a few books, a pen inside his back pocket. His mind drifts to this particular time. He remembers with tenderness, the very first time he stepped inside the walls of the university, how he was overwhelmed with disbelief and joy and definitely a sense of pride that he had finally arrived, not so much at a physical place but a state of being. He relishes arriving at a place for the very first time; this to him is always the best part of a journey. No one in his family, none of his ancestors, has reached what he has achieved, let alone been to college. He now stands before the front entrance of the university founded by the Spanish Jesuits in 1638. So much history in this university, this city, this life. He gets carried away by the moment. His mind takes him to the hallways of the academe where he sees himself walking from one classroom to another. A stellar student, his walk is one of confidence, even with a mild hint of a swagger. For Benjamin, this was the time in his life when he was at his most optimistic. As he is getting ready for his next class, he is thinking that nothing could go wrong now, with only one semester left to finish, already he feels within himself a rush of madness for his life to truly begin. He remembers the pounce of joy in his heart after he turned in his paper to the professor; it was his last exam as a student. Later that day, he treated himself to a meal of fried chicken and a few beers in one of the restaurants along Velez Blvd. After that, he went to the cinema to watch an action movie.

A sudden barrage of car honks momentarily cuts through his nostalgia, but as he looks sideways towards the busy street, he recalls the kiosk (that's what the students called it) at the back of the building. It was circular in shape, open, had benches in it, and a green roof above. He takes one last look at the grand entrance of his alma mater and makes a turn for the kiosk. It was his favorite spot, his refuge. That was where he sat while he waited for the rain to pass, or when he was too early for class. He read books there, ate his lunch, drank his coffee. The kiosk is still in place, the roof painted dark green, the benches full of Pentel pen markings—words of poetry, slogans of love and rebellion, drawings, the ramblings of youth. Benjamin sits on the bench, relieved to be away from the commotion of the street, keen to resume his nostalgia. He remembers of course that this was his place of quiet, how, despite the background of chatter from the students and the sound of cars swooshing by, he managed to distance himself from all of that. For some, the place of quiet was the church, for others, their bedroom or some other part of the house, or some place faraway, but for Benjamin, strangely, it was right there in the kiosk, accessible to noise and people. He had the ability to step out of the present situation and inhabit another state of mind. What were the ghosts, the wounds, the lamentations that took place here?

He recalls a time coming from the library when he almost cried at the thought of his mother. He seldom thought of her when he became an adult, but that Friday morning, he received news that his father could not travel to the city to attend his graduation that coming Sunday due to an unspecified illness. It was assumed that Omar was not attending either. He felt insignificant, taken for granted. He doubted his father's alleged illness and suspected that he couldn't remain sober enough a day or two before the commencement ceremony.

What kind of father would do this? Shouldn't he be sitting on the front row beaming with pride at his son's accomplishments? Couldn't he sacrifice one day of his drunken life to share this important moment with him? From this hurt, he had a sudden longing for his mother. He still treasured memories of her hand touching his forehead to feel if he had a fever, or how she always held him when they walked in public places so that she would not lose him. As a child, he had tendencies to wander off, investigating his little curiosities; a shiny pebble, a half-buried marble, a vendor selling plastic toys. He is astonished at how he still remembers that incident when he and his mother were in the market, how he casually let go of holding his mother's skirt and walked in the direction of the vendor selling balloons of various shapes while she was picking fresh vegetables. When she realized that Benjamin was no longer by her side, she shrieked and screamed his name so loudly that the market stood still for a moment and all eyes were on her. It was at this point, remembering all that, when he almost broke into tears when he sat on the bench that Friday afternoon years ago feeling abandoned by everyone. He thinks perhaps it was the sound of his mother's voice, the sound of the panic of losing a loved one that broke him. He remembers saying to himself that this was not the way one ought to live, that one should have a parent, a loved one, someone, celebrating this milestone in his life with him.

He feels less pain remembering it all now. He wonders if he will ever find happiness and would he ever recognize it. He has had moments of joy, but they were fleeting. It felt to him that his entire life was marked with a constant struggle to survive. Even when he lived a seemingly normal life in Los Angeles with a steady job and decent apartment, some sense of angst never left him, and whether that angst was caused by others or an existential one, this he has not yet contemplated. There is one childish habit he secretly still carries on, and it is that he makes a wish when he sees a falling star. He feels foolish doing this, yet he cannot help himself. As a boy, he wished something for his brother, and as an adult, wished for both his brother and father. Now he finds he deserves something for himself and it is happiness that he chooses. Is it possible to be completely happy, he asks himself, looking at the calm sky. Is it possible, after everything that happened, to begin life anew as though he was born a different person under different circumstances? What does one want out of life anyhow? What matters when you are near the end of your days, what vision and music resound, what regrets linger? He was not one who contemplated deeply about such things as soul or salvation or what it means to be alive, though he felt, two and a half years after he moved to his apartment on Keystone street, that the silence that awaited him when he came home from work was at times sad or overwhelming, and he thought, dousing the emptiness with a glass of gin and tonic or a cold San Miguel, that something was not right in his life. Strange, he thinks, to ponder life's big questions right there on the bench with the square of red azaleas to his left and pink *santans* to his right. He gives the surroundings another look—the kiosk, the scattered buildings on the campus, the old Narra trees—these images remind him of a proud moment in his life.

He has the remaining afternoon and evening to himself before he heads back to San Jacinto the next morning. Besides meeting with the lawyer, he has not made any other concrete plans. He gets in his car and drives around the city taking unfamiliar streets allowing himself to discover where they lead.

He values this moment of aloneness in the car while listening to the radio playing 80s music. He does not mind the traffic, nor the jaywalkers, nor the dreadful smog being emitted from *jeepneys* and old vehicles. At stop lights, he looks at the surroundings and finds that even with the new construction and modern buildings, some things have remained the same. For instance, the presence of a fish ball vendor, a thin middle-aged man wearing a colorful apron, cooking the fish balls in front of a small crowd gathered around his cart. In the opposite corner, an old woman is selling grilled corn, and standing right beside her is a young girl of about six years of age holding the old woman's skirt. Ladies holding umbrellas to protect their faces from the sun hurriedly cross the streets and walk to the side of the road where the tall buildings offer shade. There are two young boys begging for change from pedestrians. A young girl is selling *sampaguitas* and occasionally knocking on the windows of cars that stop in front of her.

Benjamin hears the bluster of the streets, the cacophony of urban life, and he begins to wonder if city living still suits him more than suburbia. After all, he is always pining for the quiet, the kind that is devoid of mechanical or electrical intrusions. He loves, especially, sitting on a patch of grass with a view of verdant plains or the fog circling the hills. He loves, too, watching the fading light of late afternoons. If time and distance were not a consideration, he would be near the sea every weekend. He loves hearing the stirrings of the natural world. He is this way because he is a child of San Jacinto, because early on, his sensibilities were heightened by nature more than the grand inventions of men. He is this way now, driving the streets hoping to chance upon a quiet road lined with majestic trees or a decent park devoid of a large crowd. He even fancies being

at the seaside but the one hour and forty-five minute drive in
traffic going to the nearest beach does not appeal to him. He
decides to go to The Heights, a hectare of viewing deck over-
looking the city. It sits on a mountain and is a forty-minute
drive from where he is now, on Del Rosario Street. He has been
there twice before with his classmates when they took a break
from their group study. From there, one can see a panoramic
view of the city. At night, when the sky is pristine, one can see
the lights from the neighboring island. Benjamin longs to stand
on the concrete deck and watch the dusk envelop the city.

He changes the radio station and searches for music that
is mellow or instrumental. His mood, like the sky, is chang-
ing. Random thoughts occupy his mind during the drive. It
is now two in the morning in Los Angeles, he would have
been asleep, and his alarm would sound off at five-thirty to
get ready for work at seven. He would make coffee that he
will take with him to work. If he is too lazy to brew coffee, he
would stop by Café Elan at 6:25 a.m. and not later than that
to avoid the long queue. Walking to his car, he would see the
back of a man standing in the middle of the alley and hear
him say good morning to everyone that passes him by. The
man would say, without looking at him, "God bless you", and
Benjamin's response would be to nod though the man does
not see his gesture. He misses Sang and longs for a reunion
with him. He misses Cora. He misses their interactions. In a
way, he misses the plainness of his daily routine in the States.
Oh what he would give to have a normal life, to work eight
hours and then come home and find solace there, do practical
things like making a meal or throwing the trash or taking a nap
on his comfy sofa and not be preoccupied with regret or anger
or grief. What he would do to not have such a bruised heart.

On this uphill drive to The Heights, he rolls down the window and feels the cool mountain air while the glimpse of the city is already visible. He is relieved to find the ample parking lot empty. He parks close to the store selling food and drinks. He regrets not bringing food and beer with him as he knows that the items in the store are overpriced. He pays the *tindera* and takes two cold San Miguel beer outside and heads for the nearest resting area. There are tables and seats made of concrete.

The sky is beautiful with its bright hues of yellow and orange. The sun blasts its final resplendence and signals the death of the day. For Benjamin, this remarkable phenomenon makes him believe in a god, a supreme force, mysterious, but not the sort that his religion taught him to believe. Certainly not the God who lives in heaven and created Adam and Eve. Over the years, his grasp of his Catholic faith had gone frail. There have been moments in the past when he wondered how he had lost the faith in God that his townspeople abide by steadfastly. For a while he carried a sense of guilt about it, but when the guilt banished one day, a feeling of liberation took over, for he found it a relief to no longer gauge his own actions on the standards set by an organized religion. Besides, he thought, there was a lot of hypocrisy coming from that self-righteous lot. This moment seems like a miracle to him as though he has never seen the sky burn or the sunset explode over the edge of the world. In this moment, life promises so much he could almost dream again. And for a brief moment, he does, closing his eyes and fading into another world far and different from this one. What a comfort it is, the realm of imagination that allows one to recreate oneself and others, to choose details to one's liking and break free momentarily from what one dreads. And here is Benjamin no different from when he was a boy sitting by the propped-up window of their hut dreaming of other skies, wondering of other possibilities. But this dream is short-lived, for even in his fugue state, some level of awareness abides, some modicum of practicality deters him from elation.

Evening reigns and moonlight spills upon the city below. One sees life in the dark. One imagines a tired man or woman coming home, a kitchen abuzz with the tinker of glass and utensils, the pot boiling. One pictures a household where children are doing homework or a retired couple watching their favorite television show. One speculates the conversations retelling the events of the day. One hears laughter and commotion and silence. The reality of things is what comes into Benjamin's mind when he opens his eyes. It is when the thousand sparkles of light illuminate the city that his own life comes into focus. There is heaviness in his heart of course, layers and layers of emotion that he hasn't had the time and courage to take apart.

IT CAME AS A SHOCK to Benjamin that it had been established years ago, eight years to be precise, that he was to be the beneficiary of Don Rafael's estate. Eight years ago, he lived in Sugbu city, worked at the Santo Niño General Hospital, and every other weekend, volunteered at a private clinic. Eight years ago, his life had just begun to flourish. He was grateful for what he had attained thus far: a college degree, a large quiet room that he rented from a lovely elderly couple, decent wage that he was able to stretch to send a small allowance every month to his father and brother. What else took place that year? He saved money to pay a prostitute. He was bothered that at twenty-three, he was still a virgin and his solution was to bravely walk along Solon Street where the prostitutes were commonly found, choose an average-looking woman, and take her straight to the Gold West Motel where one can pay for accommodations by the hour. Eight years ago, he treasured four things the most—his education, his freedom, that the house he lived in sat in a quiet cul-de-sac, and that his landlady prepared breakfast every day so he could eat before he left for work thereby sparing him the task of cooking in the morning or from having to spend money for breakfast at Titing's Carenderia. Sometimes he went out in the evening to dine with his co-workers. Some nights he ate dinner with the old couple who treated him like he's part of the family. At no point was it made known to him that he was the recipient of great fortune. At no point did it occur to him that this was how his life would unravel. He was not convinced that Don Rafael's generosity was out of trust and love for him as the attorney suggested. Trust, he would consider, but not love, for the benevolent gesture was Don Rafael's own act of redemption for the darkness in his heart; this is what Benjamin believes to be the case. One might ask, what if Don Rafael had genuinely grown to love him like a son? Was this not probable? Does it matter then if the love sprang from an unusual place when it was still love after all, and does this love absolve him from his sins? But one would never know the truth now when the truth is buried with the dead.

NOW HERE IS A MAN who is loyal, the most loyal in all of San Jacinto. This was what they said about Pablo. Indeed, it was true, for women, married and single, have offered to provide him comfort any way he liked it, and promised utmost discreetness, but not once did he succumb to their proposals. His quiet manner, melancholy expression, his raising two boys on his own, seemed to portray a certain kind of helplessness that won the hearts of women. His loyalty to his wife, the stubborn misplaced loyalty (she has been long dead, after all), they surmised, was what led to his depression, his drinking. Who could bear such loneliness? No one to talk to and laugh with. No one to touch. No one to make love to. No one to do anything with. For over ten years. Poor Pablo. What a sad life he's been living. And so they forgave him his drunken bellig- erence, his excessive indulgence with the bottle. Let him be, he has no one but himself. He is a sad and lonely man. Try to understand him. He had their pity. In the end no one wanted to be around him but they all tolerated his actions.

It was not entirely true that he was chaste. It was a few months after he completely stopped hearing Mass, when he felt that he lost all ties to the church and thus felt little to no guilt, that he first slept with a prostitute. This did not take place in San Jacinto but in the next municipality where he knew no one and no one knew him. It happened five times in a span of three years. It was not that sex did not appeal to him, he was considerably still a healthy man after all, but it was the effort he had to put into it that dissuaded him. The logistics, the way he had to travel back to San Jacinto on the same night to avoid any suspicions, the explanations as to his whereabouts (Omar who was then eleven years old, was always worried about him). But the truth was, Pablo was wary of any kind of relationship because he was fearful of his own slippages. He had to be careful not to confide his secret to anybody because in just one moment of weakness or vulnerability on his part, it was possible that he could commit that blunder.

He decided that the only way this mistake can be avoided was not to engage in any kind of attachment to anyone. So he kept to himself. He avoided talking to people. When he was at the town square, he bought his supplies without a fuss then hurried home. When he was eating or drinking in *carenderias,* he sat at the far end table to escape notice and attention. He became a stranger in his own town. But he wholly surrendered to the self-imposed isolation. He realized he did not need much. Drinking alone was enough. Having his best friend, Andres, was enough. Sitting in his backyard was enough. There in the backyard, he bore witness to life's unnoticed phenomena. For instance, the red feathers of the *maya,* the way the mango leaves change color from orange-pink to glossy red and finally to dark green. There he saw gaudy butterflies and smelled all day long the sweet scent of *sampaguitas.* There he knew silence intimately. The boon of a solitary life. Such quiet beauty out there. Though gloomy he had become, he loved the brightness of mornings, the way light rested on leaves and soil and wildflowers. Yes, this was enough, he declared to himself. There, where his decrepit chair stood, he was once happy.

His first intimation of happiness occurred during the first two years of his marriage before the children were born. No doubt, Aurora was the only woman he loved to the very end. Love did not have to be extraordinary to be felt, they both agreed. Companionship, warmth, respect—they had those in abundance; that was all they needed, that was their kind of love. It was Aurora's passion for plants that prompted her to build a small garden behind their hut. He learned of her fascination with bamboos. Plants thrived in her care. On weekends, they spent a lot of time in the backyard working on their garden and eating *merienda* at three in the afternoon. It comprised of fried bananas and hot cocoa. He sang *Usahay* and *Matud Mo*, his two favorite love songs. They picked names for their future children. His heart was broken for good when she died. It did not matter that he loved his sons and they gave meaning to his life. His love for Aurora was irreplaceable, unrivaled.

Two days before Pablo passed away, he did not drink any booze. He woke up at six-thirty in the morning, petted and fed the roosters, drank hot cocoa, had breakfast comprised of *pandesal,* scrambled eggs, *chorizo,* and rice. He replaced the batteries of his radio. He listened to two radio dramas called *Paglaum* which means hope and the other one called *Dear Kuya Randy* based on real life stories sent by the listeners. His old life, he mused, by which he meant his sober life many years ago where he spent his weekend mornings tinkering with the radio. Immersed on listening to *Dear Kuya Rudy,* he lay on a narrow bed made of bamboo slats that he built as his bed, but later on, had to take out of the room when Benjamin had a job and insisted on buying him a proper bed equipped with a soft mattress. He moved the bamboo bed outside and placed it under the mango tree. The heat of summer rose heavily on that early May morning, and the tree's crown offered perfect shade for Pablo. What a comfort it was to derive pleasure from a simple act of lying there bathed in the summer glow listening to the story of one Arturo Angeles. An ill-starred love story, as was often the case, about a poor man deemed unworthy to be with the daughter of a powerful politician. When the program ended, he turned off the radio and welcomed the sound of birds chirping. The story of his life, he reflected, was one of love, above all; love for his dead wife, love for his sons; love, this was what he selected as the pivotal point. For do we not somehow choose the details of our own autobiography? That he was the youngest of four siblings was one detail, that he was the first one to see his older brother dead was another. He was a farmer, an alcoholic, a fisherman, he was this and that. The details went on and on. He realized that he has agonized so much over the crime he committed that he has stopped living for a long time. What were the choices available to him that moment when he was blindfolded with a gun on his hand, and Don Rafael stood next to him telling him to fire the weapon and making guarantees that his son's future was secured? From all angles, none. It was his fate. And more than fate was his willingness to do anything for his sons' future. What he needed to do, he conceded, was to accept what has been done. Pablo, lying on his back with a view of a section of the sky, made peace with his life two days before his death. Peace finally descended, he felt it everywhere, in his heart, in the silence after the rustle of the mango leaves, in the abandoned feel of his old hut where he raised his two boys. Peace, that was his chief and final feeling.

Afternoon came without any ruckus. He brought roses and chrysanthemums to Aurora's grave. "Soon, my love. We shall be together again." He spent time by the sea. Occasionally a wave surged, and the afternoon was drenched in profuse light. He sat on the beach, his hands toyed with the white sand. The sea was as ancient as stars, he thought. A stream of life, a benediction. He was never afraid of what lurked in those depths whenever he was on the *bangka* those late evenings for the water made him feel serene. There by the sea, he also thought of his sons. There was Benjamin, the strong one, strong in thought, will, and emotion. Pablo always knew he would thrive in this world without much mentoring no matter what crosses he had to bear. When he was a child, his mind was already a vast world full of ideas and solutions, always asking what if, why not, how come. How proud he was of his son's accomplishments, especially that he was living in Los Angeles having what seemed like an important job of taking care of the elderly. It sounded worldly and prestigious given their humble beginnings. He kept the brochure of the nursing home where Benjamin worked, and was keen on showing it to anyone who inquired how his son was doing. In fact, he did not wait for people to inquire, he eagerly broached the subject. "Remember my eldest, Benjamin?" He'd offer the glossy brochure or take out the photo frame of Benjamin standing in the front entrance of the facility. He left home at an early age and Pablo felt that somehow, he never truly returned home. Yes, there were the usual visits, but even that became fewer over time. Pablo missed their conversations, their closeness. He missed his son's curiosities and turning to him for answers. He missed being a father to him. He missed being longed for. He felt that Benjamin skipped half of his childhood and leaped straight to adulthood and for this he was very sorry. He was sorry too that he failed to break open that guard that Benjamin put up as time passed and distance grew. No one could ever be that strong, Pablo thought. There must have been occasions when he got sad perhaps, lonely, afraid. Who did he seek out in those moments? Who was there for him? These topped his failings as a father; he regretted.

Pablo saved the money that Benjamin sent him every month from the time he had a job. A simple man like him had no interest in luxury or in showing off to the neighbors the possessions that he was now able to acquire. He used the money for food, supplies, and some repairs, all of which amounted to one fourth, sometimes less, of his monthly allotment. Whatever he saved he kept inside a duffel bag and three shoe boxes he hid under his bed. He set aside a sum of money for his funeral expenses that he put inside a large manila envelope which he labeled For Funeral. The house that Benjamin built for them was too big and fancy that he would have to, when time came, adjust to such material comforts. But he would remain in the hut.

And there was Omar, sweet, sensitive Omar. "Sing to me, papa, sing to me," he used to say before he went to bed. He was a delicate child, temperamental, his constitution weak. He could have been an artist of some sort with all that depth and creativity. Those beautiful ballads that he composed should be heard on the radio. Those words of poetry he scribbled on notebooks, they should have been put to good use, not gathering dust on the shelf. How proud Pablo was, he, an illiterate farmworker, to have produced an offspring with that creative talent, and whether it was by fluke or some genetic mutation or a gift from heaven, it did not matter. How he missed those times when Omar played his guitar every night before he went to bed. How exquisite it sounded, and how it brought him to tears. Pablo wished he were an encouraging father to him, or that he expressed his thoughts openly, then perhaps, Omar would have turned out to be an assertive person, maybe even ambitious. Perhaps. If only Omar was not easily impeded by life's cruelties, he could have focused on making a career out of his creative inclinations instead of running away, moping, and daydreaming. For what else did he do when he disappeared for long periods but mull over misfortunes that cannot be undone. Pablo believed that Omar blamed himself for his mother's death, that he did not, could not, forgive himself. He was burdened with this unnecessary guilt, this has always been his private battle. It did not occur to Pablo that that one night more than fifty years ago was where the damage occurred. If only he was not too inebriated to notice that his son was awake and overheard his entire confession. It never occurred to him to recant his statements or say that it was all drunken talk, that there was no truth to any of his prattle, especially not the part about him being a murderer. He could have easily persuaded him to dismiss those thoughts; after all, Omar was at that age when he believed everything his beloved father told him.

Omar, his favorite child, the one who will never leave his side. Bless his heart. They have had arguments, normal arguments between father and son. All things considered, they managed to live harmoniously, never mind that their accord was characterized by pure tolerance and lack of honesty. Pablo did not conceive of any rift between his sons. Not his two boys who grew up close and protective of each other. No, he wouldn't tarnish this impression. His memory was filled with their boyhood games and silly exchanges, their affection, all these in the midst of their poverty. Their brotherhood love was the only certainty that gave him comfort in the last years of his life. He will die believing in this unwavering fraternity.

He was sixty-nine years old, but he felt that he has lived more years than that, ten years longer. His body agreed with this assessment. Years of laboring at the farm under any weather conditions and the heavy drinking had worn out his body. If he were to consider that every heartbeat of grief, pain, and oppression was taking away years in one's life, then he was lucky to have reached his sixties. At his wake, someone said that he died of a broken heart, that the diseases listed on his death certificate were all plain formality. In the end, the person said, what the living will remember of the dead is the story of a life. And Pablo's, they recalled, was composed of gusts of grief and loneliness, and in between, the abiding love for his sons. Whenever people passed by the hut, they pictured Pablo sitting on the bench under the mango tree, gathering up his young boys, his arms wrapped around them, telling stories of myths and folklore and how this world began.

A month before Pablo passed away, Don Rafael came to see him unannounced. He sat next to Pablo who was lying on his bed. He held Pablo's hands and asked for forgiveness. Throughout the town's history, no deity has ever succumbed to such humility. Pablo had tears in his eyes and said nothing, quietly still acknowledging his place in the world which was that of a servant and the man before him was his master. From their pulses, they revealed the depths of each other's emotion, and within the fifteen minutes of silence between them, an unlikely sense of brotherhood transpired. In the eyes of their god, they were men of equal footing, not one superior or inferior over the other, bound together by their wrongful acts of which both paid a price.

A month after Pablo passed away, Don Rafael went to all the churches of every place he went to, knelt from the entrance all the way to the altar muttering "God forgive me for I have sinned." He made his confession directly to God instead of a priest for he did not want to reveal his mortal sins to another human being. He coveted a *compadre*'s wife, forced himself on at least fourteen women. He orchestrated the assassination of two business rivals. Both victims survived. One became paralyzed for life and the other lost his right eyesight. The hired assassins were from another island and no evidence was ever traced back to them or to Don Rafael. He couldn't forget the names of five men whose deaths he had been responsible: Edwin Reyes, Jose Alfonso, Arturo de la Cruz, Crispin Adlawan, Raul Santiago. He lit a candle for each of them at the Basilica del San Agustin, the same church where his private confession with his god took place. He knelt in front of the statue of Jesus nailed to the cross. He thought of Pablo, acknowledged that he had caused him much suffering, but his remorse went only as far as taking advantage of his vulnerability and hopelessness, a poor farmer at his mercy, a sad man with nothing to his name who will do anything for his sons. Then, he thought of Benjamin, and feelings of tenderness towards the boy, the closest he had to having a son, made him feel guilty.

He had not known guilt until he went to Pablo's funeral. It was as if death had been the catalyst. It moved him to witness the grief that Benjamin and Omar felt. Ever since he stood under the scorching sun with men and women crying unabashedly and praying for Pablo's soul to go to heaven, he felt a change within him, something he could not identify at first, only that he recognized how easily simple things moved him. The sound of children laughing almost made him weep, the church bell on Sundays, even the sight of a woman carrying a child. Tragic events reported in the newspapers upset him, so he only read the business section. After his morning coffee, he took lone walks down the road past his property. People were shocked to see him walk around without any bodyguard. Is he not afraid of getting assassinated or abducted? They wondered. The probability of a gunman taking him down in the street at daylight did not concern him any longer. He greeted everyone good morning. When he saw a child, he reached for his wallet and handed the child money. Please, take this money for your food and clothing. He gave away every cash and change he had in his pocket. He thanked God for sunrise and clean air. He thanked Him for his functioning limbs and strong knees, his still perfect eyesight and teeth. Why this sudden appreciation? Initially he thought it was old age that turned him sensitive. But a week after he took a final glance at Pablo's face inside the casket, his past transgressions began appearing in his dreams. Faces of dead people haunted him in his sleep. He saw the faces of victims as they pled for their lives. He heard their wives and children scream. He woke up sweaty and anxious that he stopped taking *siestas* and dreaded going to bed. He vowed to atone. He made a list of every single thing he was grateful for, and each night before he went to sleep, he prayed and thanked the Lord for each item on his list. He erected a tennis and basketball court for the youth at remote *barangays*. He donated computers and books to public schools. He gave large donations to religious charities.

He was in Calamba city on the day of the wild storm to personally hand a check to the parish priest of Our Lady of Fatima church. The amount he gave was the biggest donation the church had ever received. It was a little after one in the afternoon when the day turned eerie. He had just come out of a restaurant when dark clouds descended, and animals of all kind became unruly and were heard letting out all sorts of sounds as though sensing the impending doom. The wind picked up all kinds of litter then dumped them all over the avenue and beyond. The sky was at its most somber. He stood in the corner smoking a cigarette, detached from the proliferating commotion before him for what was chief on his mind had nothing to do with the afternoon turning gray but how alone and lonely he felt; he finally understood what it meant to be a human being, and he realized how he failed miserably, and that, no matter how large his monetary donations were, that would never be enough to redeem his soul. He threw the cigarette butt on the street and walked headed east when the first drops of rain began to fall.

OMAR WROTE HIS INITIALS on the guitar that he took with him on the night he left home for good. He laid it on the sand but not close enough for the water to reach it. He wanted to leave something behind that could perhaps give people a sense of his last whereabouts. Inside the guitar was a note he addressed to Benjamin. A stranger, high from sniffing glue, walked along the shore and stole the guitar thinking he can pawn or sell it for a couple of pesos. The stranger threw away the stapled piece of paper that was inside the sound hole. Omar's note said, "I do not blame you anymore. It took me years to understand, but when I did, it was too late. Live life for us. I am proud of you. I miss you, my dearest brother. I love you."

Benjamin will never know that those were Omar's last words to him. He will also never know that during those years when he was living away to attend school in the municipality of Borja, Omar celebrated Benjamin's birthday by going to the bridge near the sugar mill that they used to frequent when they were children. Omar would say a prayer for his brother and wished him well despite his resentments towards him. He would throw a couple of pebbles into the water like they used to do as kids. "Oh, Benjamin," he would mutter to himself while shaking his head, then he would head back home. Benjamin will never know that when Omar was in fourth grade, a classmate, Pedro Colina, told him he ought to be ashamed that his father, Pablo, was the town drunkard. Pedro told him that he and his mother saw Omar's father asleep on a bench one early morning while they were on their way to the market. It was clear that he passed out drunk. This embarrassed and upset Omar to the extent that he pushed his classmate; then he ran outside and went straight home before class was over. When he reached home, he lay on his father's bed and feigned sickness. He did not tell anyone what happened, especially not his father no matter his prodding and scolding. He never went back to school again. Ever since that day, Omar lived in his own private world, one that belonged in the mind. He was capable of going on for days not speaking to anyone. To his father he gave one-word answers; sometimes a nod or a shake in the head. To the outsider he was aloof, strange, impenetrable. Those were the years when life for him took place inwardly, full of secrets. What were some of his thoughts? He thought of the story he overheard from the grownups talking about how his mother almost drowned when she was a young girl. The specifics were vague, only that she was on a *bangka* that capsized, and that a fisherman saved her. Who was she with? Why was she on the *bangka*? Was she traumatized by it? Was this the reason why he was afraid of the water? It's a shame, really, because he did love the sea, loved its vastness, loved how it connected islands. He wondered how deep it went, what sorts of creatures thrived in those depths.

He thought of Benjamin's sleeping quarters at the mansion, perhaps he had a queen size bed with a soft mattress, big pillows, a lamp on an elegant side table, a dresser with nine drawers. He was not jealous of his brother's newly found comforts because somehow, he knew that in exchange for all of that, he had to attend school. Omar would gladly sleep on the floor each night and not be mandated to sit in the classroom all day with those dreadful students. He checked the garden after his father left in the morning, and watered the plants when the soil was dry. He talked to the bamboo plants on occasion, greeted them, and asked how they were doing that day. This simple task of tending the garden gave him pleasure. It afforded him a sense of place in the world for he felt that he did not belong in the classroom like other children. When it rained, he stayed indoors and read the two school books he had, one science, and the other civics. He practiced reading the words aloud, page by page. He collected any reading materials he found on the streets and took them home for practice reading on a rainy day.

His self-imposed vow of silence ended when Arturo, his *Tio* Andres' youngest son, took him to a basketball game that took place in the plaza. "Just come and watch. Sit for twenty minutes and see if you enjoy it. If you don't, you can go home if you want. You don't have to talk to anyone." Omar watched the entire game. He cheered. He sighed, he laughed. He felt overwhelmed by the crowd's thunderous applauses, the whistling, the screaming; he treasured all of it. When he arrived home, he told his father that he wanted to play basketball. Then began a new phase in Omar's life. He turned out to become a celebrated three-point shooter, a crowd favorite. He was sought after by many teams from different *barangays* which enabled him to visit other areas and travel from the northern to southern tip of Sugbu. Those, perhaps, were the best years of his life. At some point when he was nineteen, he stopped playing basketball. He felt that there was nothing more to achieve. Learning to play was a want, being good at it was a challenge, but winning trophies was a feat he did not conceive was attainable. He surpassed his own expectations. He was content.

One evening, he found himself in the company of a man strumming the guitar. Omar was passing by when music wafted from the church grounds where the man with the guitar sat alone. It was impossible not to be stirred, impossible to keep on walking. Omar paused and stood still under the palm trees, under the brilliant evening sky that often made him feel at once joyous and melancholy. He listened to the music, and felt that the people who passed by the church grounds and ignored the music, or those who were nearby sitting on the benches gossiping, or those gallivanting in the town plaza, deprived themselves of experiencing something beautiful. How many times in a person's life does one experience something utterly sublime, almost miraculous as this? It was as if the musician's body had a voice, and this voice came in the form of music, for it was not only his hands strumming the guitar that created the music, but it came from something poignant as though it came from the depths of his soul. The man was completely immersed with his music, playing as though he had reached a zenith. Omar, in absolute awe at what he witnessed seemed to have also reached a certain depth which he held was akin to a rarefied communion, a spiritual experience. Omar was keen to be the man's audience, so he moved closer and sat a few yards away from him. His name was Basilio. He did various work for the church like gardening, simple carpentry, and any other errand that Padre Carlos asked him to do. He said he salvaged the guitar from a church patron who threw away the instrument. "Sacrilegious," he said. "I don't know much about anything. I can't write or read. But what I do know is that music nourishes my soul." Twice a week, they both met in the same church grounds where Basilio taught Omar how to play the guitar.

"You're a natural, Omar."

"I don't think so. Perhaps it's just my strong conviction to learn."

"No, I've taught a couple of people in my life, young and adult alike. I recognize talent when I see one. I want you to have this guitar. Whenever you feel sad or lost, play some music and it will make you feel better."

OMAR WAS TWENTY when he first stepped foot in the city. It was his birthday present to himself. He planned it two months in advance. He made inquiries about accommodations from former basketball teammates who have been there before. Upon arrival in the city, he checked in at Wilson's Pension House, then went to the city's main library for he wanted to look up photos of plants and find out their names, genus and characteristics. He also looked up historical sites and tourist spots. Among the list of places written in the books and brochures, he visited the Taoist Temple, Magellan's Cross, and Fort San Pedro. He spent two hours loitering and praying inside the Carmelite Monastery. He was delighted to find that one could write one's wish on a piece of paper, drop it inside a box, and the nuns would go through each paper and pray for the wish to materialize. He relished his time in the city and understood the allure it had on his brother. Since then, he visited the city two or three times a year. He used some of the money he saved from the allowance that Benjamin sent for him and their father every month. In one of his trips, he went to Benjamin's university and toured the campus. He passed by the boarding house Benjamin took residence when he was a student. Walking cleared his head, so he walked and walked as far as he could until he got tired.

A loner at heart, he never came close to having a friend that he could confide in. Even when he was young, his preference for company was selective and mood-based. He retreated to solitude. On his lone walks, he took notice of plants and trees that he passed by on his meanderings. It was with nature where his thoughts found a home, for indeed his thoughts were abundant and deep, and perhaps brimming with confessions that disclosing them to another human being would be revelatory of his inner angst. And yet, though peace descended upon him from the sight of the green expanse of sugarcanes, or from the memory of him and his brother exchanging laughs, or from walking home on evenings guided by the light from stars; no matter where his mind strayed, his thoughts always came back to that particular night when he was a young boy woken up by his father's raucous voice.

That evening was lodged in his memory forever. He thought he heard his father crying. He lay still on the floor, his eyes blinking in the dark. The noise did not abate. He stood up and peeked through the open window. The whole town was bathed in moonlight. The full moon lit the roads and walkways, even the darkest of nooks were exposed. He saw his father and *Tio* Andres sitting by the mango tree. He quietly opened the door, and their voices became audible. He stood there listening to their conversation. "I murdered someone, Andres." "This is the sin I committed." He has never seen his father in that inconsolable state before, and all that Omar could do was cry. Nothing in the world could ever make him forget that night for he was the sort of child who does not forget. He knew that to kill was wrong, though he was unsure how he came upon this knowledge. Perhaps he learned it from one of Padre Carlos' sermons. Why would his father kill when it was against the teachings of the church? His mind did not comprehend his father's act, but what he knew with certainty that night was that his father committed a sin.

He was twelve, twenty-three days away from turning thirteen, when he fully grasped what his father had done. By then, he knew by heart the Ten Commandments. One afternoon, a group of boys at the basketball court talked about a friend's acquaintance who was stabbed to death. They described in detail the victim's multiple wounds, blood spatter, the location of the body, the motive of the crime as though they were little detectives. Omar listened to the entire conversation and felt pain in his upper abdomen. What was that pain, that shudder in his body? It dawned on him that it was the shock, the disgust of his father's terrible sin, a crime that could imprison him for life if the authorities found out. Walking home from the basketball court that late afternoon, he tried to reconcile the two sides of his father—one the murderer; and the other, the loving one, the epitome of tenderness. He had never even yelled at him and Benjamin when they got into mischief as young boys. He had not seen him get angry. Not once has he laid a finger on them so how could he have managed to kill someone? Besides that, did he not fear God? Love God? Believe in God? He broke the sixth commandment, his beloved father, the one who preached to them the Catholic values they should abide by. Such hypocrisy! Also, did he ever go to confession? Is he remorseful? What act of contrition has he done? When his father stopped going to church, Omar went to Sunday Mass by himself and stayed on after the Mass was over. He cherished the quiet after all the parishioners had left the church. He conveyed to God his confusion and angst.

"I murdered someone." Sometimes those words appeared in his mind unprovoked. They intruded at any hour whether he was preoccupied or idle. They haunted and distressed him. But no amount of profound devotion to the church gave him comfort. He found this to be an anomaly, a disappointment. In later years, he would contemplate his sustained adherence to his faith, question life, question everything.

Omar carried his father's secret, and did not speak of it to anyone. It was no wonder then that he kept to himself, that when he found things to be unbearable, he walked and sought nooks of peace among trees and spent hours lying on the ground watching birds and butterflies and paying attention to the movement of natural life around him. Peace and beauty at last, he often thought. He made note of the uniqueness of each leaf and pebble. He watched the movement of caterpillars and bugs. He whistled when the birds sang. Sometimes he spoke out loud. Sometimes he cried. Sometimes he fell asleep for hours. And he prayed, he let out his pain and anger and found peace in the silence that greeted him after every outburst. During that period when Rosario was in his life, he took her to these gentle places. He brought a basket packed with egg sandwiches and iced tea. He plucked a mix of bougainvilleas, *kalachuchi*, and wildflowers, and handed them to her. They were in love. He had never felt happiness of that sort. He felt fortunate to have found love, he, who was shy and did not think much of himself. He did everything he could to keep their relationship even though it meant that they had to love in secret. No doubt Rosario's boyfriend, a corrupt cop with a penchant for violence, would have killed him or her for that matter, had he found out about their affair. He sang to her. They wrote each other letters. They rendezvoused in the city. When they went there, their customary way of travelling was for Omar to take the 8:15 a.m. Ceres bus at the town square. Rosario waited for the same bus that stopped at a station in her town. When she got on the bus, she did not sit next to Omar. She did not nod, smile or wave to acknowledge their acquaintance. They pretended not to know each other to escape suspicion in case someone from her town was also on the same bus and would spread rumors about her being involved with another man, or worse, the person might go straight to her boyfriend and tell him of her deceit.

One day when Rosario failed to show up at the bus stop nor at Café Nicole, their designated place of meeting, Benjamin did not agonize over whether something was amiss, but rather, his instinct told him that the day of their final parting had arrived. At first, he assured himself that perhaps she was late and took the next bus, but the hours passed and nightfall came, and still there was no sign of her. He waited until nine in the evening, then wrote a note for her and left it with the cashier who had come to know both their names and faces over time. Omar walked to the motel feeling defeated. His brain warned him from the start, that even though the joy in her eyes was evident when they were together, that even if once or twice they thought of eloping and moving far away, yet their time together took place only in moments and those moments were going to have an end someday. His logic told him that this parting could happen any time without warning or announcement, but his heart did not heed these admonitions; his heart was happy and brave to love under these circumstances. Oh, his heart, his heart. It was possible that it was his greatest strength but also his most fatal flaw. He knew that she would leave even though they were deeply in love, for this parting had nothing to do with love but with practicality. He accepted that he could not match the material offerings her boyfriend provided her with and as did her family, nor could he guarantee the possibility that he could do the same. Though Omar was devoid of viciousness, he also lacked ambition. He would go to the deep woods to gather rare flowers and give them as a gift for no special reason, he would serenade your evenings and recite impromptu poetry, but it would not occur to him to plan for the future. He would drift for hours and get carried away with wild imaginings, but those thoughts wouldn't include finding ways to earn money or pursue an education. It wouldn't include concrete plans of how he intended to support Rosario and where they would live. To him their love would quell all adversities; they would find a way to live; they would manage. It was a given then that Rosario couldn't be with a man like him as sometimes in this part of the world, love alone did not suffice, not if the weight of being a provider for a family of six was put on your shoulders. Poor Rosario, Omar thought, to be the eldest and hold the duty of looking after the welfare of her parents and three siblings; poor Rosario to be young and beautiful and unfree; poor Rosario to have to forsake her own longings.

Those were his thoughts when he walked to the motel carrying a duffel bag that contained three shirts, underpants, and the usual bouquet of flowers that he picked from an open plot of land half a kilometer away from home. He thought about how they met. It was at a fiesta in a barrio whose name he could not now recall. What stood out for him was this demure girl who wore a long, flowered skirt. The circumstances of how they were introduced had become vague in his memory. He just remembered her smile, her shyness, how she looked misplaced in the company of girls who were talking and giggling loudly as if seeking attention. It was the little things, the specific details about her that he would miss the most. For instance, the chaotic lines on the palm of her hands, lines, she said, that foretold of the disappointments and adversities that would plague her life. She would cry then, and he would spread out her hand, trace every line, convince her that each represented a fortune that awaited her. This line for remarkable health, that for prosperity, the other for finding the great true love, etc. He fabricated them of course, only to stop her from crying. He would miss her letters, her handwriting, the way she wrote the words all in capitals, and underlined the words love and happy, and I am yours forever. He would miss the way she picked three songs every month for him to learn on the guitar, and ask him to play all of them when they were together. His life would change from now on, he thought. He would have to live with the memories that would accompany him wherever he went—the meadows, under the awning where they first held hands, the sunny rooms of cheap pension houses, this beguiling city and the very streets that he walked on.

The deepening night imparted its usual murmurs. Omar longed for privacy in his motel room and checked in hurriedly. It was when he placed the flowers next to the lamp that he began to feel utter sadness. He cried quietly. He despised life's cruelty. He succumbed to self-pity. He felt that he reached the most disconsolate tier of aloneness. He slept turning away from the street lights that shone through the window, away from the mad world that carried on indifferently to his fate.

He decided to remain in the city for two more days and did the customary things he would have done if he were there alone. He thought of his mother. When he was twelve, he realized that he possessed nothing of her, not even a memory. But one morning, he found a necklace half-buried near one of the bushes at the far end of the garden. It was an ordinary silver necklace that had a cross for a pendant. He showed it to his father who asked him where he had found it. But without waiting for a response, Pablo proceeded to say that that was Omar's mama's long-lost necklace, and how bizarre that it was just right there all along as though it was meant to be found by him. Never mind that this was not true, never mind that Pablo made up the story to put a smile on his young son's face, a little white lie wouldn't do him harm. Omar never took off the necklace from the day he first wore it. He had something of his mother's, at last.

On his last evening in the city, he went to a seedy night-club that had go-go dancers. He thought this was going to be a pleasant distraction. A woman sat next to him, keen for conversation and maybe more. The initial talk consisted of the exchange of customary information—name, place of origin, whether one was alone or expecting company, might one like to dance. The woman remarked that he had beautiful eyes and how neat he looked. She rambled about things that were of no interest to him, things that had to do with her new Seiko watch, her crazy roommate, personal details of the regulars at that club. Sitting there half-listening to the woman, the more he thought of Rosario. The pleasant distraction he thought he would have did not occur as instead he felt strongly how empty his life was. He longed to find his way into the world again but nothing in his immediate environment helped. Not the thump of the music, not the sashaying of bodies nor the glitter of disco lights. He did not finish his second drink. He walked ten blocks to get back to his motel. The walk calmed him. He took pleasure in looking at the shabby buildings downtown, the lampposts that lit the street revealing the spectrum of city life in the dark. There were the vendors pushing their carts to their next destinations, the homeless setting up their tents, people seeking diversions. He walked with wonder and with sorrow. He wouldn't come this way again. He would seek other paths and forget this one.

The first thing he did when he arrived in his motel room was throw the flowers in the trash. He couldn't wait to get home to San Jacinto. The days that followed reduced him to a more somber mood witnessing his father's drinking. It came to the point that his father started drinking right before noon without eating any food. Some days he left the house at ten in the morning and came home in the evening drunk. Omar would ask his father if he ate and his father would shrug and go to bed. Worried about his condition, Omar made breakfast so that it was available to his father before he began drinking. Pablo ate very little, and sometimes the food remained untouched. Omar felt as though his father was slowly slipping away from this world and only remnants of him remained, while the ways that he recognized his father took place when he was asleep at night for his snore was unmistakable, or early morning when he fed and petted the roosters and was still sober. But in between those two occasions, his father was either a stranger or a ghost.

During the day when his father was at home, he spent it sitting on his wooden chair in the garden. He stared at the mango trees. He sat unmoved, drinking while the hues of morning, afternoon, and evening changed before him. Sometimes he whistled or hummed a tune. Omar often looked at his father from the back door of the hut and found the sight of him there from morning until evening to be both moving and tragic. Omar could not bear this feeling, so around noon he took his walks and left his father alone. Between them there was a world of distance and silence and lack of confrontation. Each went on his own divergent course. His sense of duty towards his father was so strong that he never thought of leaving home. Who will take care of him? Who will make his meals? Who would force him to eat? Not that his father was senile and needed to be looked after, but still, Omar knew that his conscience wouldn't bear it if anything bad would happen to his father. Who would notice if he hasn't come home, or was missing? Who would look for him? What if he died in his sleep? So Omar never left home even if home was not exactly a cradle of refuge. No, home was the anxiety of opening the door not knowing the state his father was in. Home was gathering all the empty bottles of liquor scattered on the porch or in the garden, and putting them in the bin. Home was lying down on a cold bed praying that he and his father would make it to another day without difficulties or disaster.

During this period, Omar composed twenty-five songs, wrote twenty-three poems, and read thirty-two books. He planted eighteen seeds of various kinds all over town and wrote in his notebook the exact location of each seed. One late evening as he was walking home, he felt a sudden pang of pain that made him pause. It was not the pain of heartburn or exhaustion or hunger, but the weight of loneliness. He thought, is this life, the emptiness flowing through every vein of your body? Is this life, these gusts of grief, the bursts of pain?

After his father's death, a profound void loomed. Now that everyone he loved was gone from his life, his parents, Rosario, even his brother Benjamin, Omar felt a new kind of emptiness. A sort of exhaustion of the spirit took over that forced him to stay in bed until noon, waking up only to eat lunch and take a pill for his headaches. Daylight hurt his head, so he stayed indoors for as long as possible, stepping out only to buy essential supplies, and occasionally visit his *tio* and *tia*. He could have made use of his new freedom—he no longer had to care for his father or watch him suffer—to live life anew or reinvent himself, yet he could not establish a footing. Many believed he was consumed with grief, and though this was true what they were not aware of was that he had always been plagued by a mysterious suffering that encompassed his entire existence, and whether this began at birth by the death of his mother, or the estrangement from his brother, or the gravity of his father's secret, only Omar knew. He lingered in bed in the afternoons while the rest of the town carried on with its usual flurry and preoccupations. Sometimes tears fell from his eyes as he lay on his bed. He felt that nothing awaited him out there; he had no one and he belonged to no one.

There is no comfort in the material world. I envy the dead. Those were the last words he wrote in his notebook.

BENJAMIN IS DRINKING his second bottle of beer, reveling at the majestic view. He feels like an old man in his 30s, weary from what he has lived through, that his yearnings have been reduced to gazing at the harmless stars and relishing his drink without any disruption or incident. A past revisits once more. He recalls the very first time he set foot in this city. The three hours he spent tagging along with *Manong* Ramon running errands on the busy streets of Colon and Echavez was a big moment in his life. It was not so much that he had a reason to gloat and became the envy of the farm boys that he had been to the big city, but that the throb of joy in his heart was distinct and unforgettable, and in that moment, his ten-year-old self had made a decision that one day he would move away from San Jacinto and live in the city.

Years later, when he moved there to attend the university, he felt the same sense of elation. But what he also felt, tucked away quietly like a well-guarded secret, was simply the gladness of being released from what he found disheartening in his life. He found it unbearable to witness his father's helpless resignation, and if he were to be utterly honest, he would acknowledge the embarrassment he felt, gathered amongst other people, when the talk was of fathers and their careers and legacies. He detested the simple-mindedness of the townsfolk, their lack of ambition, the turning to gossip and intrigue, the obvious lack of quality of life. These were the reasons why there was a time when he did not mind being away from home, when San Jacinto became just a place where he used to live. There were even moments when he despised the little details of existence there, despised especially the irritating crow of roosters too early in the morning, the dominant smell of fire in the summer from the burning of sugarcanes, the sting of mosquito bites, the stray dogs that shit everywhere. When he came to America, it was the ultimate dream realized, having foremost in his mind, the dollar, and second, the countless opportunities. It was there that he experienced the power of money, the material comfort it afforded if he worked hard and saved. He loved the first world pleasures it gave him. He relished them so much that for a time, he thought he could not live in San Jacinto again, could not imagine waking up to the vacant silence of endless plantations or spend afternoons looking at the dusty road that presented nothing but the weary faces of farmworkers going home. He could no longer stand the absence of cinemas and coffee houses, the lack of clean public lavatories, the potholed roads that were not fixed until the campaign season for the next election began. He dreaded the parochial views, the trivialities. No, he wouldn't have that life again. But such is the complexity of the heart and mind, he realized now, probing his own life with intensity, having for company the silence of the night and the sheer unfolding of his own thoughts. What was true then was true only for a time, for even though Sugbu and Los Angeles have served him well, after a while, he felt misplaced. He was an anomaly, a man who was at once at home and elsewhere, and even his own shadow was familiar yet also strange. Yes, he loves both cities but there was something about them that made him feel lonely, and when he felt that way he found himself wistful for San Jacinto again. He forgave its flaws. He reckoned it to be a gratifying place to live. He defended its people. What is it about a man, who, having finally arrived at his place of longing finds that he belongs somewhere else? He is abashed at his failings, his flightiness, but somehow, his own honesty consoles him. He contemplates having a third beer, the last one, while deciding what to do with the rest of the evening.

Benjamin's rage abated after Don Rafael's death, though there are moments in the deep night when the noise that he hears is the sound of Don Rafael's helplessness, his last gasp, and Benjamin catches himself clenching the object he is holding in his hand to the point of breaking. He feigned sickness to skip his funeral. To make it credible, he stayed in bed and wrapped himself with a blanket even though it was a warm day, and asked his *Tio* Andres to go to the pharmacy and get him Biogesic, Immodium, and some guavas and oranges. Three days after the burial, he went to Don Rafael's grave to spit on it and he call him names. He vandalized the headstone using a big black Pentel pen, wrote the words Evil! Scumbag! After he was done expressing his anger, he went to his father's graveyard. He squatted on the ground with his head bowed. For a brief moment he felt sorry for himself, contemplating the details that were kept from him all those years. He would have loved to hear the revelation straight from his father, no matter how macabre and raw the details, and not a secondhand account from *Tio* Andres. He wanted to know, for instance, if the murder took place that same day when he heard his father cry in bed. Had he forgiven himself? Found peace? Then he imagined what it must have been like for his father to carry the secret all those years, to rise each morning and resume his duties as best he could without showing the tears in his eyes, the decay of his mind or the corruption of his soul, as the same pair of hands that toiled the earth and raised his sons to be decent human beings were also the very hands that took someone's life away. How did he manage to live with his daily compunctions? How did he sleep when his inner chaos battered loudly against the quiet of evening when he retired to his makeshift bed? Alcohol, of course, Benjamin finally understood. He imagined what his father must have felt when he chided him for his drinking, when the way he looked at him at times showed his disappointment and waning respect. How he must have hurt his father's feelings. He had very few regrets in his life but this one topped them all.

He lit a candle and spoke to his father. *Papa, forgive me, that for a time, I was so full of myself, felt that I was above you and everyone else here because I breathed the clean air of foreign cities, walked their well-paved roads, experienced their commerce, industry and first world machinations, had more than a glimpse of their perceived greatness, while you, each day, wiped the sweat from your brows and brushed aside the ache in your body, an ache that not only came from years of hard labor but also from your quiet despair. Forgive me, that for a time, I looked at you with disdain because you didn't make much of yourself and I blamed you solely for your failure. After your brother died, your father died two years later in an accident. It was another tragedy you had to cope with at a young age. Your mother worked part-time to feed all of you and take care of your younger siblings. You too had to put food on the table. Your dreams were deferred because duty came first. Duty, papa, was sacred to you. Forgive my arrogance, my myopic lack of comprehension. I have come to realize that a man's greatness is to be measured, above all, by the profundity of his love, and your love for us, your children, was proof of that. You were a poor man, but I am poorer than you. I have travelled to many places yet no matter where I go, no matter how far away, I always think of home, here, where, as a young boy, I used to daydream about those other places. Here, where you lived your entire life bowing to the soil that sustained you and received your heart's lamentation. Here, where the waters nourished you and gave you peace, while you were out on the deep sea hoping for a good catch, so you could feed your sons. Out there at sea, you were quietly dreaming of a life that was not always oppressive. I know what you had to give up so I can have the life I wanted. I am living that life because of you. Yet I feel lost, empty, because you are not here, Omar is not here. I know what you did for me, papa, and ultimately it cost you your life and my brother's life. But redress was obtained. Your deaths have been avenged. Don Rafael is dead.*

BENJAMIN STARES at the brilliant sky and remembers a time when he loved this world, loved every minute of being alive. It had to do with this sky, the awe of beautiful mornings, the sallying forth of new life that expelled the old. It had to do with hope and benevolence and deliverance. God, whoever you are, god of light and hope, give me the courage to live, he mutters to himself. Give me the courage to live, so much so that when I drive the car and go back to my motel room, I shall dispel all dark thoughts. Give me the courage to remember that I have a nephew waiting for me. Give me the strength to live because I have to raise him. His father is dead, and his mother is nowhere to be found. Bring me back the future that I once lived for.

"Sir, excuse me, is this your wallet?"

Benjamin examines the contents, surprised that the wad of cash is still intact.

"Yes, it is. Where did you find this?"

"On the floor, sir. You must have dropped it. Be careful, sir. There are a lot of pickpockets. They even steal your cellphone."

"Ah, careless old me. Thank you, boy. Here, take this. For your honesty." He grabs a couple of twenty peso bills and gives it to the boy.

"Thank you, sir. My sister is sick, and I can buy some soup for her and medicine. God bless you, sir."

Benjamin is moved by the boy's blessing more than his honesty. Children, he thinks, are the only good people in the world, pure in heart and spirit, incapable of inflicting pain. The boy made him think of his nephew.

Alonso asked if he could come with him to the city. He was tempted to say yes, but decided against it. "It is only an overnight trip but when I come back, you and I will take a road trip," Benjamin assured him. "We'll go to Kawasan Falls, the hot spring in Catmon, explore some caves. We'll stop at every place we fancy and go island hopping." Benjamin had every intention of fulfilling his promise, especially after seeing the joy in Alonso's eyes when he mentioned the road trip. This consoled him, gave him a sense of purpose.

JUAN BELIEVED HIS GRANDSON, Alonso, was a magical boy; no doubt a miracle, a gift from heaven. A couple of times Juan thought he was going to lose him to bouts of pneumonia, fever, and rashes, but the boy miraculously survived any and all illnesses without the service of doctors. He survived by consuming broth, ginger root boiled in water, and fresh coconut juice straight from the fruit. Guava leaves, *malunggay,* and *atis* restored his immune system. The boy had an unexplained affinity for the sea, and he would request his grandfather to take him there especially when he felt something was amiss.

"What is it, Alonso?"

"It's my chest and nose, *Lolo* Juan."

The boy would go into the water and stand still once it reached just below his knees. He would take deep breaths as if he was inhaling something emitted from the depths, as if a sacred communion took place between him and the sea. Juan looked at this act of subtle exchange with strange awe and wondered how on earth this became part of his grandson's senses. Who told him to do this? How did he know what would make him feel better? Who gave him this idea? Certainly not him, nor Alonso's playmates. Juan believed that there were mysteries in the world that no man or science can explain, and this was one of them. For indeed the boy had a sense of innate knowingness as though souls that lived and relived since time began were fused into one, and this composite that carried all the knowledge gathered from many lifetimes dwelled in his small body. It was true that he dreamt of his father. Four times, in fact. All four dreams involved the sea. He and his father swimming or his father walking on the shore carrying him on his back. He did not tell anyone that he dreamt of his mother as well, a dream that foretold of her death and in which case he strangely understood that she was no longer in this world. For his uncle Benjamin, he feels utmost tenderness. He knows his grief. His *tio* appears to be strong, yet his moments of vulnerability are given away easily in simple gestures if one is observant and perceptive. He had noticed, for instance, the way he blinked his eyes or lowered his gaze to the ground when his papa Omar's name was mentioned, for his name was sometimes another name for death, or brotherhood, or love. He noticed too the way his uncle's voice cracked when he told him of their boyhood stories, especially the one that involved the haunted tree and the bridge by the sugar mill. He noticed how often his uncle visited his father's grave, twice a week, sometimes more. He knew it was his father's grave he visited because he brought a can of beer with him, and when he visited his mother, he brought flowers.

At night after his *tio* put him to bed, he sat in the garden and drank beer or some other beverage. Sometimes when Alonso was unable to sleep or woke up to drink water or go to the toilet, he peeked through the window and found his uncle still sitting there. He wondered what his uncle's thoughts were in his evenings of aloneness, if he was sad or at peace or worried. If only he could alleviate his troubles and tell him that he shouldn't worry too much about their plight. He had never felt unwanted but there are days when he could not help but wonder if his uncle was overwhelmed or burdened by his presence, or perhaps, if there was a part of him that longed to leave everything behind and resume his life in America. After all, his arrival in his uncle's life was sudden and unannounced, and for a single young man who lived his life on his own terms, he was rightfully unprepared for such a responsibility. But he tried his best to instill some sense of normalcy into their lives.

In a short span of time, they had to discover things about each other, and this was initially achieved by asking Alonso what food he wanted to eat, what activities he felt like doing, if he slept well, if he was feeling all right, if there was anything he needed. Alonso, for his part, thought it best not to bombard his uncle with inquiries that may provoke uneasiness or enlarge his sadness. He did not ask, for example, why people die or what sort of accident his papa Omar died from. Instead, he asked what his uncle's favorite toy was as a kid, if he loved to swim, what his favorite color was. He asked if he had a girlfriend waiting for him in America, a question that made his uncle grin. Meanwhile, he is aware of his simple tasks. He abides by what he is told to do without any resistance. Take a shower in the morning, finish the food on his plate, brush his teeth, keep his room tidy. He is given freedom to explore the surroundings provided he tells his *tio* where he is heading, north towards the sea, or south towards the town square. He is encouraged to speak whether it is to ask a question, express a need, a confusion, an ache in his body, or a plain declaration of his thoughts. There are moments in the early afternoon when he attempts a *siesta*, that he thinks of his papa. He thinks of him not so much as the ashes in a jar, but as a person, an adult version of himself, once possessing the faculties of all his senses, once capable of laughing and crying and thinking. He thinks of him too as a boy, roaming the same land that is the site of his own daily wanderings. Whenever his feet touch the soil, he feels a connection with his father, his ancestry, and all the history that runs through his blood of which he knows nothing about.

He ponders what to do with the ashes. At present the jar rests on a book shelf in the living room, within his reach, so he can move it to his bedroom or anywhere he pleases. He has no wish to scatter the ashes, not for now at least. In his papa's room, there are open boxes that pique his curiosity. There he sees posters, notebooks, comics, letters. In those plain boxes are fragments of his papa's life. Though he does not know how to read, he recognizes his mama's name written on the envelopes. Those letters, he thinks, are evidence of his parents' love. He shall read them one day and keep them. He will know them more intimately. A small photograph of his mama sits on top of his drawer. Every night before he goes to bed, he bids her goodnight as he does his papa. He is not a religious child. He knows God or the concept of God. Sometimes he prays. Each morning after breakfast, he checks on the bamboos, waters them as needed, inspects them for flowers. He wants them to bloom, he longs for good news. He is hopeful.

BENJAMIN STANDS UP and stretches his back, readying himself for the drive to the motel. He approaches the edge of the viewing deck and leans on the thin railings, the only barrier between where he stands and the deep ravine. He is about two thousand feet above sea level. Lights from the far island continue to shimmer. For a moment it seems to Benjamin that the flashes of light are from the boats on the waters of San Jacinto, and he is standing on the shore looking out into his beloved northern sea; the sea his father ventured onto alone at night; the sea that cradled his father with its invisible wide arms and blessed him with sufficient catch; the sea that was also the sole witness to his brother's last moments; the sea that received his body then washed it ashore. At once Benjamin feels small and magnanimous, victor and loser, scared and courageous. Then strangely he feels as though a large swell is lifting him up to a lofty height, as if Magwayen, the goddess of the sea, summoned the spirits of his loved ones, his father Pablo, his mother Aurora, and brother Omar, and all four of them are briefly together, happy. Benjamin blinks his eyes and finds his feet standing firmly on the concrete. He feels relieved, and alive, fully alive, and shaken first at what his consciousness just experienced, and second, at the distinct throb in the folds of his heart, pulsating heavily as if saying to him: live, live. He does not know that just three days ago, an accident occurred on the very same spot where he now stands. A man fell to his death when the railings he held on to collapsed. He does not know that what Sisa also saw when she looked at the palm of his hand years ago when he was a boy, was that the final tragedy of his life would be his own death in an accident involving heights, and it would take some benevolence, a kind of mercy, a form of intervention from the gods for his untimely death to be thwarted. It appears, without his knowledge, that he had earned that dispensation. And here is Benjamin, dutiful son, loving brother, survivor, hero of his own story, a lone figure walking under the immense sky. History-maker, vessel of all things sad and beautiful, beacon of hope for generations to come.

"Alonso, it's time for bed."

"I'll be there in a little bit, *Lolo* Andres," he replies, looking out of the window waiting for his uncle to come home, as the deepening night envelops the town where this story began.